ARS
HISTORICA

ARS HISTORICA

MARIE BRENNAN

First published 2017 by Book View Café Publishing Cooperative.
304 S. Jones Blvd. Ste# 2906
Las Vegas, Nevada 89107
http://bookviewcafe.com

Print edition 2021
ISBN 978-1-61138-953-1

"And Blow Them at the Moon" was first published in *Beneath Ceaseless Skies*
#50, August 2010. "The Deaths of Christopher Marlowe" was first
published in *Paradox* #12, April 2008. "Two Pretenders" was first
published in *Beneath Ceaseless Skies* #60, January 2011. "The Damnation of
St. Teresa of Ávila" was first published in *Shared Nightmares*, ed. Steven
Diamond and Nathan Shumate, November 2014. "To Rise No More" was
first published in *Beneath Ceaseless Skies* #207, September 2016. "False
Colours" was first published in *Wilful Impropriety: 13 Tales of Society and
Scandal*, ed. Ekaterina Sedia, April 2012. "Dying Old" was first published
on An Archive of Our Own, December 2012.

CONTENTS

FOREWORD

There are five basic schools of thought on the topic of author commentary in a short story collection: 1) put it all together at the front; 2) all together at the back; 3) individually before each story; 4) individually after each story; and 5) don't bother.

For the ebook editions of these collections, I can leverage the format to facilitate multiple approaches, by linking to the notes at the end of each story while collecting the notes themselves at the end of the book. Alas, dead trees are not so flexible, which means I have to pick. You will find all the story notes following the Afterword, and can time your reading of them as you choose.

This collection contains seven stories, all of them either historical fiction or historical fantasy. They are set in different time periods and different countries (though the majority of them take place in England), and range in length from a pair of novelettes all the way down to a piece of flash fiction less than six hundred words long. I thought about putting them in chronological order, but eventually discarded the notion; the resulting order is quite random. I hope you enjoy them!

AND BLOW THEM
AT THE MOON

Henry Garnet's breathing was the only sound inside the room, marking the passage of time like a ragged and desperate clock. Everything else was remote, muffled, the street outside as distant as a foreign land. He knelt with both hands clenched white before him, trembling as his lips shaped the words. *Domine, adjuva me.*

Soundless as those words were, they sent a faint chill rippling across Magrat's skin. But she stayed and watched, because she'd made one mistake already, and didn't want to make a second.

It was hard to know the right path, even after all these years. Once she'd been the grim of Hyde Abbey, and her duties had been simple: she haunted the church—a task that would send most faeries shrieking for safety—and rang the bell on occasion, and knew which dead were destined for Heaven or Hell. But the abbey was gone, along with all the other monasteries, and English Catholicism was reduced to this: priests in disguise, creeping from house to house, saying Masses in the blind hours of the night for their tiny recusant flocks.

She could have found another home. Occupied some new-built Anglican church, or fought another grim for his established place. Instead she followed the Catholics, and most particularly this man, who was Father Superior to the Jesuits in England.

Henry Garnet could not see her. Magrat doubted he'd appreciate her presence; Jesuits were a passionate lot, their faith enough to try even *her* endurance, and they didn't look kindly on the notion of faeries. And that was her excuse, inasmuch as she had one: it would have been harder to pass unnoticed in the garden. She was no woodland sprite, after all. So she'd stayed indoors, when Garnet invited the distraught Father Tesimond to walk as he confessed, and had therefore missed what Tesimond had said.

Whatever it was, it put Garnet here, on his knees in this cramped little room, tears tracing bright lines down the weary planes of his face.

He never liked coming to London. In some ways it was safer here; a man could easily vanish among the tens of thousands of mortals packed within the city walls. Out in the countryside, the searchers knew which houses were likely to harbour priests, and hunted them relentlessly. But the city was also the source of that threat: just upriver lay the chambers of Parliament, who passed laws telling England's remaining Catholics the many things they were forbidden to do. Garnet was a gentle soul; he preferred to keep distant from politics, trusting in Providence to vindicate his cause.

That trust had clearly taken a sharp blow today. What had Tesimond *said?* Some new law, perhaps, or the torture and execution of yet another priest—

No. Before they went into the garden, Tesimond said he'd heard someone's confession recently.

"Blood and Bone," Magrat said between her teeth. Garnet was so lost in prayer, he wouldn't have heard her even without the charm that cloaked her presence.

Confession. She'd followed the Catholics for decades, as the various recusant families married one another, bore children, grew to old age or died before they could, and so on to a new cycle. She knew them: the children who learned their catechisms in secret, the wives who concealed priests and then lied to the searchers, and the men.

The men, who chafed at the restrictions of Parliament. Who eagerly anticipated the toleration James would grant once he had claimed the throne of England, and who cursed his name when that toleration proved merely the King's usual ambivalent diplomacy, careful promises that committed him to nothing.

The men. Some of whom had rebelled with the Earl of Essex four years ago, before old Queen Elizabeth died.

Some of whom might do so again.

A second curse formed on Magrat's lips, but died unspoken as a cold wind brushed over her soul.

Garnet's breathing had stilled, where he knelt upon the floor.

Magrat stared at him, holding her breath in unconscious echo of the priest. He'd done something—*decided* something—

And now he was going to die.

A church grim could taste death, scent it on the air, feel it in the marrow of her bones. Every mortal carried a little bit; death was always a possibility, from accident or disease. But sometimes the possibility grew stronger, closer, when a man stood at a fork in the road, then chose the path that led toward peril.

She could even guess what Garnet had decided. A faerie couldn't shadow Jesuits for years and not learn a few of their ways. Anything said in confession could only be shared with the permission of the penitent: Tesimond had gotten it, but Garnet, she was certain, had not.

However tempted he might be—whatever reason he might have—he could not break the seal of the confessional. That was the conflict that had gripped him since Tesimond left. And the strange peace on his face, as he turned it up toward Heaven, told her what choice he'd made.

He would keep the secret. And because of it, he would die.

Might, Magrat thought, as the priest murmured a conclusion to his prayer, rose, and left the room. *He* might *die.* At some point in the near future. And that was none of her concern.

But this was what came of following Catholics. It was easy to watch mortals come and go, from the security of a comfortable church; much harder when she lived in the shadows of their lives, seeing their dedication and courage in the face of persecution. Also their flaws, their missteps and mistakes—but that, too, was part of knowing them, and knowing was a dangerous thing.

It was a short step from *knowing* to *liking.* Sometimes even *admiring.* Things no church grim should ever feel.

She should let this go. Her duty was simple: if Henry Garnet died at the hands of the Crown, hung or burnt or drawn and quartered, then his Jesuit brethren would come in secret to witness. And if the eyes of one drifted past the scaffold to the shadows that lay beyond, she would show him whether his Superior was going to Heaven or to Hell.

Only that, and nothing more.

But she'd left her duty behind in the ruins of Hyde Abbey. Everything she'd done since was choice.

And she liked Father Garnet too much to let him die.

She chose instead to save him from his fate.

The Onyx Hall, London: 24 August, 1605

It was almost like being in a church again. The long gallery that led toward Magrat's destination was a high, narrow thing, its ceiling a row of pointed arches; add windows of coloured glass, and an altar at one end, and she could imagine Father Garnet saying a Mass here.

At least until the inhabitants stopped him. This was no holy ground, but rather a faerie palace, and its people did not take kindly to prayers.

In the normal way of things, she would have been with him. It was the Feast of St. Bartholomew, and the Jesuit was at White Webbs; he and the ladies of his congregation were considering a pilgrimage in secret, to a holy well in Wales. Garnet's fear seemed to have faded. He'd written in vague terms to Rome, saying he feared some violent action against the King, begging for the new Pope to forbid it; that was all he could do, and apparently he believed it would be enough.

It wouldn't. The death hovering over him proved that. And so Magrat, for the first time in years, abandoned the priest she'd appointed herself to follow, and came here instead.

The gallery ended in a humble door, bronze-bound and low

enough that taller fae would have to duck. Magrat pushed it open and stepped through into a place that was very nearly as unchurchlike as it could be.

The first thing she heard was a voice swearing in a thick Cornish accent. "Can't even dig a tunnel straight, ye thickerd—I told you 'twas sloping up, and so it was, right into someone's cellar—"

A scattering of faerie lights and tallow dips lit the wide, low-ceilinged room of the Crow's Head, shedding their uneven glow across the heavy tables and benches. The tavern's few occupants were a motley sort: one stick-boned sprite, giggling quietly amidst empty wineskins; three cloaked figures radiating silence in a shadowy corner; and nearest the door, two knockers, one berating the other without pause for breath.

The tavern's owner, a hob named Hafdean, was busy at work beneath the preserved human head mounted on the far wall. A platform raised him up high enough to wipe down his bar of beer barrels and wine casks; he was smaller than Magrat by a good foot, and ugly enough to make her goblin features seem plain. He tossed aside his rag as she approached and squinted the wrinkles around his eyes even deeper. "I've seen you before. Church grim, female, old-fashioned clothes—Magrat, isn't it?"

She put one hand defensively to the tattered dress she wore. Old-fashioned? Perhaps so; she'd taken it from the body of a woman refused consecrated burial, before the abbey was destroyed. But this was the Onyx Court; the fae here liked to copy mortal habits, in dress and other things, and Magrat's usual rags would have gotten her laughed at just the same.

"Yes," she said, in answer to Hafdean's question. The hob raised a cup and a questioning eyebrow, but she shook her head. "I didn't come here to drink. I'm looking for help."

"It don't come cheap," he warned her.

Of course it didn't. This was what happened when faeries gathered in anything so organised as a court: they whispered and schemed and bartered their favours to one another. And since gold and silver meant little to them, the price of those favours took a different form.

"I've bread," Magrat said. "Baked by a Warwickshire kitchen maid, who was beaten when her mistress learned she was tithing to the fae." The last loaf was stained with a bloody fingerprint and damp where the maid had cried, bidding farewell to her faerie friends. Magrat had fought the local sprites to claim that one.

Hafdean nodded. Mortal bread protected against mortal banes, which made it the most precious thing in all the Onyx Hall. These fae lived beneath London itself, and few of them had a church grim's tolerance for church bells. And iron, of course, hurt everyone. "What is it you need?" the hob asked.

"Someone who can look into a mortal's dreams, and read what lies there."

"Whose dreams?"

Magrat winced. But truly, had she expected Hafdean not to ask? Someone would have, sooner or later. "A Jesuit priest's."

His laughter echoed from the tavern rafters, knobbled beams like old black bones. "Not for bread, no; not for the heart of Mab herself. You're mad if you think anyone would try."

Not mad, just desperate. She didn't know who'd confessed to Tesimond, which meant the priests were presently her only sources of information. "I think some Catholic is planning something," she said at last.

Hafdean managed to look down his lumpy nose at her, even though his platform put them at equal height. "I remember more than just your name, Magrat. I remember the first time you came into this tavern. Full of grand statements, you were, how faeries shouldn't meddle in mortal doings. Now here you are, asking just that, because now you've found something you care about. A *Catholic* something, at that."

Venom dripped from the word. Fae didn't care a rush for the points of doctrine that divided mortals, but they did care about the effects. Catholic rituals had been around a long time; they'd worn channels in the fabric of the world, strengthening their power against faeries. The hot faith of puritans could be just as bad, brute force acting in time's stead, but the Reformation was a good thing in the eyes of many fae.

Particularly those of the Onyx Court. Living as they did beneath dozens of churches, of course they favoured anything that made it easier for them to walk outside.

Magrat didn't want to debate religion with the keeper of the Crow's Head. Instead she used the other obsession of these London fae. "If there's Catholic trouble, it means trouble for everyone. And your Queen doesn't want that, does she?"

Hafdean scowled. Magrat had never seen the Queen of the Onyx Court, but she knew the tales: Lune had sworn to work for the good of England and its people. She even ruled with a mortal man at her side, the symbol of her pledge to live in harmony with his kind.

Secret harmony, of course. Even besotted with love, as rumours claimed, Lune wasn't mad enough to think fae could announce their presence beneath London and survive. If her subjects wanted to meddle, they had to do so in stealth.

Grudgingly, Hafdean said, "Could be Parliament's ruffled someone's feathers. But they've been out of session because of plague. Won't meet again until..." He leaned past Magrat. "Gommuck! When's Parliament sitting again?"

The knocker who had been complaining when Magrat came in said, "The fifth of November."

Hafdean jerked one calloused thumb at the mining spirits. "They'd know; they've been in and out of Westminster for the last year. Trying to make their own faerie palace over there, if you can believe it; but all they have to show so far is a half-finished tunnel. Ran out of bread, which makes it hard for them to work. If you want help, you could pay them."

Magrat cast a dubious glance at the pair. "Are they any use?"

Hafdean snorted as if swallowing a laugh as loud as when she'd spoken of Jesuit priests. "They're the most incompetent knockers in all of Cornwall. Think digging a hole in the ground, with shovels and their bare hands, is the way to build something like this." Hafdean's gesture took in not just the Crow's Head, but everything beyond it: the Onyx Hall, miles of galleries and passages and chambers great and little, all enchanted against iron and faith and the curiosity of mortals.

Well, she didn't need their architectural skills. The knockers looked up hopefully when Magrat approached. They were knobbled things, and well-covered in dirt, but they listened eagerly as she made her offer: bread in exchange for the whereabouts of certain Catholic gentlemen, when they came to London.

Perhaps she couldn't get information from Tesimond or Garnet. But if she found the penitent who made the original confession, she wouldn't have to.

Gommuck puffed out the chest of his filthy doublet and said, "We'll find 'em for you. Anyone you want us to start with?"

Magrat bared her teeth in something like a smile. She knew *exactly* where to start.

"Robert Catesby."

Westminster Palace, Westminster: 2 September, 1605

Unfortunately, Robin Catesby was the one man they couldn't find.

He wasn't the only one to have ridden with Essex in that failed rebellion; his cousin Francis Tresham had been there, too, and Tresham's brother-in-law Lord Monteagle. But Monteagle was too cautious to court danger on his own, and Francis had always followed his cousin's lead, even though Catesby was the younger by several years. *Everybody* followed Catesby's lead: he inspired without trying, through his reputation for courage, his potent charm, and the blazing light of his faith.

Gommuck and his friend did find another Catholic for her, though, a fellow Magrat knew well. Thomas Percy had leased a house near the knockers' tunnel, within the precinct of West-minster Palace, an edifice nearly as sprawling as the Onyx Hall itself. The choice made sense: Percy had been made a Gentleman Pensioner last year, one of the bodyguards to the King, and there was advantage to being so near the chambers used by Parliament. But when Magrat went, under cover of a glamour and with a piece of bread to protect her, she found someone else living there, a man of Percy's named John Johnson.

Johnson was a tall fellow, red-haired and strong; he looked more a soldier than a servant, and the eye he bent upon Magrat was very warlike indeed, when she asked where Percy could be found. "What do you want with my master?"

Fortunately, she had an answer prepared. The mortal man who ruled the Onyx Court alongside Lune was also a Gentleman Pensioner, in his public life. "I come on the business of Sir Michael Deven," she said.

The glamour disguising her was of an ordinary varlet. Respectable enough, but Johnson's frown deepened. "What business?"

"None of yours," Magrat said, trying to think of a way to question him without being stabbed for her pains. She'd felt it the moment he opened the door: the spectre of death hovered over this man, as over Father Garnet. Which meant Percy had probably fallen under that shadow, too.

"Anything that concerns my master concerns me," Johnson said, crossing his arms. The chamber behind him was dark and cramped, even by the standards of Westminster Palace; she couldn't imagine what Percy would want with it, and certainly he and Johnson could not both live there at once. Not in a style befitting a gentleman's dignity.

The servant saw her looking and shifted to block her view. Magrat wished she'd made her glamour as tall as he was, but did her best with the height she had, matching him glare for glare. "Sir Michael will hear of your interference," she said.

The prospect of a knight's wrath apparently did not trouble Johnson. He shut the door in her face.

In the narrow passage outside, dank with the smell of the nearby Thames, Magrat sighed. Truthfully, she would tell the Queen's consort nothing. Even presuming she could gain access to him, he wouldn't appreciate her free use of his name, and even if he let *that* pass…the man was a Protestant, and shared Lune's opinions on religion and the fae. Neither of them would help her save a Jesuit priest.

No matter how kind and generous that priest was. No matter

how much he desired peace, or wished to be a faithful subject to the King. All they would see was Catholicism, and stamp it out.

Johnson was only a servant; it wasn't worth the cost of having someone delve into his mind. She needed Percy, or better yet, Catesby. And if the knockers couldn't find those two for her, she would have to hunt down people who could.

Gothurst, Northamptonshire: 17 September, 1605

"His father left behind tremendous debts," Anne Vaux said quietly, walking along the moonlit terrace of Gothurst with her hands clasped at the small of her back. "Poor Francis' inheritance is not at all what he hoped."

She could not possibly have meant the words as an accusation against her hidden listener, but Magrat winced anyway. This was the cost of her absence: she'd missed the death of Francis Tresham's father, and the funeral. If she had a duty in these churchless times, that was it; but she had missed it, because she was chasing this secret instead.

At least she'd found Father Garnet again. The pilgrims had returned from Wales and were dispersing once more to their homes, scattered across the midlands of England. Since the Treshams were in mourning at Rushton, Garnet had come here, to the home of Sir Everard Digby, with his dear companion and protector Anne Vaux.

Mistress Vaux was no fool. She'd concealed Garnet from searchers for ten years and, through her family, was related to half the Catholics in England. She could not see death as Magrat could, but trouble was plain enough to her sharp eyes. "I noticed Robin was not at Rushton to comfort his cousin," she said, as they came to the end of the terrace.

"He is...much occupied with his affairs," Garnet murmured.

Hah, Magrat thought, from her uncomfortable perch in a tree. Jesuits were not permitted to lie outright, but they had many ways of avoiding the truth. That one wasn't even particularly subtle.

Catesby *was* planning something.

Mistress Vaux noticed it, too. "Affairs that might explain the horses I saw being gathered at the houses of my cousins and friends? Horses fit for war." She'd come outside without gloves, but Magrat didn't think the twisting of her pale hands was born from cold. "Father...I feared these wild heads had some scheme in mind, and now you confirm it. I beg you, for Heaven's sake: you must speak to Robin."

"I have," Garnet said, clasping her hands in his own. From another man the gesture might have been intimate, but Magrat understood; Anne was his sister in Christ. Deep as the bond between them ran, it held nothing impure. "You needn't worry, my dear. Robin merely seeks a military commission in Flanders. He's made friends with a soldier named Guy Fawkes—or Guido, as he calls himself, as he's been fighting for Spain. With this peace between England and Spain, 'tis legal enough; Robin's even asked me to write a recommendation for him, to the Archduke."

Magrat missed Anne's response, distracted as she was by the sudden whirl of her thoughts. Flanders? That would never have put Garnet into such desperate prayer. But perhaps she was wrong; it might not have been Catesby's confession that Tesimond heard. She'd just assumed it, because of what the man was like.

Even if his intent *was* for Flanders, it did nothing to help Garnet. And Magrat doubted the story anyway.

As did Mistress Vaux, she saw. "And what of the horses?"

Garnet shook his head. "Perhaps others are planning to go with Robin. They might do better abroad, exercising the heat out of their blood—though I would hate to lose any in war."

He wanted to believe it. They'd held a secret Mass a few hours after midnight, and now, a little while before dawn, the peace of it remained with him. At moments like this, with the practice of his faith fresh and his beloved sister at his side, Henry Garnet was a happy man, and Magrat didn't want anything to darken that.

But a shadow moved across the face of the moon, eclipsing its light, and Anne Vaux shivered when she looked up at it. When her hands slipped free of his and she went two steps away, still looking upward, Garnet said, "Shall we go inside and pray for them?"

For a long moment, Anne did not answer. Then she said, distantly, "No. I had rather hear you sing, Father. I fear we'll have little time for it, soon."

Magrat's own skin tingled at her words. Anne might just mean the end of their pilgrimage, the return to the demands of everyday life, which did not often leave time for Garnet to exercise his fine voice and skill with the lute. But it took on a more ominous cast, because Magrat saw all too clearly the death that still haunted the priest's steps.

It lay some months away yet. But still there. Waiting. To silence forever that delightful voice, the music in those dextrous hands, and chill all the warmth of his heart.

Garnet smiled at his protector. "We will always make time for song. And I will write to Lambeth. If any wild head *does* plan something foolish, I shall persuade Robin to tell me of it."

Magrat almost missed it, in the preposterousness of thinking that man would be persuaded to anything. Garnet had, quite casually, given her the answer she'd been seeking all this time: where Robin Catesby could be found.

If either the priest or the gentlewoman remarked on the sudden shaking of a nearby tree, Magrat did not hear it, for she was already gone.

Lambeth: 2 October, 1605

At first she thought it was Thomas Percy all over again. Magrat found the house Catesby was renting, but he wasn't there. She recognised the gentleman who was, though: Robert Keyes, another Catholic, and another man beneath the shadow of death.

How far did it *reach?*

Any doubts she had were erased when Keyes received a visitor from across the river. Percy's man Johnson came by one afternoon, and Magrat, listening from the roof above, heard Keyes call him

Guido. This, then, was the soldier Garnet had mentioned, Guido Fawkes. Whatever he was doing in Westminster, hiding under a false name, it had nothing to do with military commissions in Flanders.

So she stayed, trusting that her quarry would come to her eventually. It wasn't pleasant waiting; she'd spent enough bread paying Gommuck and his friend Scalliock, and protecting herself on the trip to Northamptonshire and back, that she couldn't afford to eat any now. As it stood, she could either pay someone to read dreams, or hoard the remainder to use once she had her answers; she could not do both. Fortunately Lambeth, across the Thames from Westminster, was thinly settled enough that she could mostly avoid iron—and it would be a sorry day indeed when a church bell knocked a grim unconscious.

She waited, and her patience was repaid. Robert Catesby rode in shortly after noon on the second of October, just as the light changed.

Gommuck and Scalliock had babbled about this, when she gave them their payment; something about asking the Queen and her consort for permission to try a charm on their tunnel during an upcoming eclipse of the sun. But she'd clean forgotten, even after that night at Gothurst. Magrat was watching the street from behind the house's chimney, leaning out every time a rider approached; and so intent was she upon her target that it took her a moment to realise the sun's light was growing dim.

It seemed to split Catesby in two, the man and his shadow—and not the shadow he cast upon the ground. A church grim could gaze upon the souls of the dead and know whether they were destined for Heaven or Hell; now, in these peculiar moments of eclipse, it was as if that sight applied also to the living. She saw the bright Catesby of glory, tall and strong, the man whose cousins and friends looked to him for hope; while Father Garnet might be content to wait for Providence to rescue the Catholics of England, this man would forge Providence with his own hands and the white-hot fire of his faith. But she also saw the Catesby of shadow, whose desperate devotion to that cause respected no boundaries, not even those of Christian decency. *That* man would endanger not just himself but everyone around him, as he flung himself from the precipice of chance.

She was right. He stood at the heart of it. This was the mortality Magrat had sensed around the others; if they died, it would be because of Robert Catesby, and whatever madness he planned.

The light brightened once more. If Catesby had even noticed the eclipse, he gave no sign. He dismounted, then led his horse around to the back, calling out quietly for Keyes. Magrat, shaking off her paralysis, scrambled forward until she hung perilously over the roof's edge; but the two men inside spoke too quietly to overhear.

And she couldn't approach. Not without bread. Forget Jesuits; the passionate faith blazing in Catesby now was worse than any priest. He could burn away a charm of concealment without so much as a word, just by the thoughts that possessed his mind. There would be no reading his dreams, not for the heart of Mab herself.

Magrat pulled back, her stomach churning even from that brief encounter, and withdrew to a stack of firewood a safe distance away. Keyes was too close to Catesby, with passionate faith of his own. What she needed was someone less devout, someone trustworthy enough to share Catesby's secrets, but unreliable enough to betray what he knew.

She thought of the interwoven trees of Catholic families in the midlands, and a fierce smile curved her lipless mouth.

She needed Francis Tresham.

Clerkenwell, London: 24 October, 1605

She finally ran him to ground in Clerkenwell, after chasing him halfway to Northamptonshire and back. Tresham had been in the city, but gone home to fetch his mother and unmarried sisters, bringing them down to London.

It made little sense. His family was all in mourning still for his father. Why bring them to the city, where death's grip slowly tightened around all the men of his circle?

Of course he could not sense that death; but he knew his cousin was up to some mischief. Magrat was sure of it the moment she crawled through his window and heard him tossing in his sleep.

She took care to move silently. Tresham was not alone, when she pulled back the bedcurtains; his wife was a dark, unmoving lump at his side. But her husband's thrashing did not wake her, nor the moans and whimpers that issued from his throat, and so Magrat decided to proceed. She might not get another chance.

Closing her eyes, Magrat summoned the image in her mind.

She'd decided, after much internal debate, to leave Tresham's dreams untouched; it did her no good to spend all her remaining bread on knowing his mind, only to have no way to act on the knowledge after. And what if Catesby had *not* confided in him? Deception was cheaper, and worth trying first.

When the illusion of her glamour was in place, Magrat hissed, "*Francis.*"

Tresham jerked as if at a gunshot. But memory served her well: he was a poor sleeper, easily caught on the boundary between dreaming and waking. That was where he hung when he opened his eyes and saw the figure of his cousin, standing at the foot of his bed.

"Robin," Tresham mumbled, somnolence slurring the word. "What—"

"You were screaming, Francis," Magrat said. "Why?" Her mimicry of Catesby's posture and manner of speaking was imperfect, but the more nightmarish this encounter, the better. Poor Tresham—there was no uncertainty in the darkness that marked him. This man *would* die, and soon. No matter who won: the Catesby of glory, or the Catesby of shadow.

Tresham's eyes were open, staring; he'd drawn his knees up, like a child, until he hunched against the pillow. Next to him, his wife breathed quietly on. "'Tis damnable, Robin—we'll be damned for it—"

"Damned for what? What are we going to do?"

Too direct. His throat worked convulsively. "Wait, Robin, please. At least until we know what they'll do. To strike on the first day—perhaps 'twill not be so bad as you fear—"

Who? What first day? Magrat gritted her teeth, searching for a better tactic. "We *do* know, Francis. I've told you before: this is the only way."

"At least let me warn Will. And Ned." Tresham clutched at the blanket, as if trying to rein in a runaway horse.

Will—that was likely William Parker, Lord Monteagle, husband to Francis' sister. Which made Ned Edward, Lord Stourton. Another brother-in-law. "What warning would you give them?"

"To stay away!" It had the sound of a shout, strangled down to a bare whisper. "They mustn't be there when the King comes."

The King. Two lords—the first day—

Tresham was talking about Parliament, which James would reconvene in less than a fortnight. On the fifth of November.

Thoughts flashed through her head, of rebellion, prisoners, hostages. Magrat had to try the words three times before they would come out. "And what of the King?"

His shoulders drew inward: a small boy, cringing under the harsh gaze of the cousin he'd adored since childhood. "I'll do as you bid me, Robin. No matter how far it goes."

Tresham's wife was stirring; Magrat didn't dare stay. She moved swiftly to Francis' side, looming over him. "Then I bid you be silent. Or you will suffer for it." And she let her glamour slip, revealing the horror of her goblin face beneath.

He screamed and flinched back. In that instant, Magrat vanished into the shadows; then, while Tresham's wife thrashed into wakefulness, she slipped through the window and closed the shutters behind her. Let him think it just a nightmare, brought on by his fear.

Fear born of a very real cause.

I'll do as you bid me, Robin. No matter how far it goes.

She could guess at how far. Not for nothing would Catesby have gathered such men around him: staunch Catholics, good swordsmen, and soldiers like Guido Fawkes. And he would lead them to salvation, or into Hell itself.

This was the secret Father Garnet knew, and could divulge to no one. Robert Catesby would strike at the King during the opening of Parliament. How he expected that to do any good, Magrat couldn't guess; whether they threatened James, or took him prisoner, or—her stomach curdled—*killed* him, it could only poison everyone's hearts against the Catholics. But she'd seen that bright aura during the eclipse; somehow, there was the chance of glory.

And also the chance of disaster. The black hand of death stood ready to take them all. If Magrat wanted any Catholics to emerge from this unscathed, let alone one Jesuit priest, she had to take steps toward that end *now*.

Hoxton, London: 26 October, 1605

> *My Lord out of the love I beare to some of youere frends I have a caer of youer preservacion therfor I would advyse yowe as yowe tender youer lyf to devys some exscuse to shift of youer attendance at this parleament for god and man hathe concurred to punishe the wickednes of this tyme and thinke not slightlye of this advertisement but retyere youre self into youre contri wheare yowe maye expect the event in safti...*

A few rambling lines, written in Magrat's best handwriting. Too little, and yet too much; anyone who could be proven to have known of this plot in advance would be in a great deal of danger. But it was the best she could think to do. Garnet would need a protector, someone who could hide him or even spirit him out of England; Mistress Vaux would not be enough. And so Magrat lurked in the shadows, trying to muster the nerve to approach Lord Monteagle's house.

He, at least, was likely to survive whatever came next—so long as he stayed clear of it.

Hesitation turned out to be useful policy. A man was approaching along the street, a servant she recognised from her previous visit to Monteagle's house. Before fear could trap her, Magrat hurried out into the street.

The servant stopped, warily, one hand hovering as if to draw a knife. Magrat had disguised herself in a tall man's seeming and a cloak; too late, it occurred to her that she looked like a cutpurse.

She spread her hands wide as she approached, displaying the letter she held. "A message for your master," she said in a low voice once she drew near. They were alone on the street, at least for the moment, and in principle there was nothing wrong with delivering a letter; but fear had half stolen her voice.

She offered the folded paper. The servant eyed it, still wary. "From whom?"

"A friend," Magrat said. Still he hesitated, until she said, "*Take* it, man. 'Tis only a letter, and meant to do him good."

He snatched it with a quick hand, keeping as much distance as he could. Magrat said nothing, and neither did the servant; he merely jerked his head in a quick nod and continued on his way. And she let out a long, ragged breath, hoping her meddling would pass unnoticed.

When five figures melted into view around her, she knew it had not.

Magrat whirled, seeking an exit that wasn't there; any of the five would grab her before she got far. The goblins were unfamiliar, a barguest and a thrumpin, but she recognised the other pair: Gommuck and Scalliock. And the fifth, to her surprise, was a mortal man.

He appeared young, but some of that was a lie; just as she could feel the shadow of death's hand, so too could she feel its absence. A touch of faerie kept age from this man. He might be years older than the thirty or so he appeared to claim. His doublet was as dark as his carefully-trimmed beard; the dull colour helped the charm that had hidden him and the others. But it was cut of good cloth, with decorative stitching unnecessary to its purpose, and the sword at his hip marked him a gentleman.

In quiet, measured tones, the man said, "What was in that letter?"

"I don't have to tell you that," Magrat said, even though she suspected she did.

The goblins were drawing closer behind her. The man, not blinking, said, "I am Sir Michael Deven, and you have spent enough time in the Onyx Hall to know what that means. I ask you again: what is the content of your letter to Monteagle?"

Thrusting her chin belligerently forward, Magrat told the Queen's consort, "I warned him away from Parliament next week."

"Why?"

He asked as if he didn't know the answer, but Magrat had heard far too much about the Queen's spies to believe it. In which case, why not tell the truth? They'd have it from her, one way or another.

"Because Francis Tresham wanted it," she said. "To keep him safe. I have letters for the others, too—Stourton, Northumberland, all the rest of the Catholic peers, or the ones sympathetic to them. It'll be better if they aren't there."

With every nerve drawn tight as a bowstring, Magrat was alert to the smallest movements: the shift in the barguest's weight, the indrawn breath of the knockers, and the curling of Deven's left hand into a fist. His right hand remained loose, ready for the hilt of his sword. "So you knew of this," he said flatly. "You knew, and chose to warn the Catholic peers—but not to warn *me*."

Gommuck started to say something, but Magrat gave him no chance; her anger broke loose, like a dam giving way without warning. "Why should I?" she demanded. "I've smelt the death around these men. Can you say honestly that you wouldn't kill them, or tell the King's men and let *them* do it instead? They've a right to make their grievances heard. It pleased James well enough to pretend he would be a friend to Catholics before he came to the throne, but now that he's King in England it pleases him to forget he ever said anything. Patience hasn't gotten them any toleration. I've watched Father Garnet pray for it for years, on his knees to the Almighty *begging* for their freedom, but that has gotten them *nothing*. Maybe this won't, either, but at least they're trying something!"

Deven's nostrils flared, and one foot slid forward into a fighting stance. For a moment Magrat believed he would snatch out his blade and stab her right there in the Hoxton street. Instead he said, through his teeth, "You're a church grim. Tell me: how many of the dead would go to Heaven, and how many to Hell?"

"Dead?" Magrat blinked, not understanding. Unless he had a church grim in his service, she didn't know how he could be aware of that. "Catesby's men? I won't know until they've died—"

"Not Catesby's men," Deven spat. "The King. The Queen. Prince Henry, and Prince Charles, all the Lords Temporal and Spiritual and the House of Commons besides, and everyone else unfortunate enough to be within half a mile of Westminster Palace on the fifth of November, when the gunpowder blows. How many souls to Heaven, and how many to Hell, for the freedom of your Catholics?"

Magrat's eyes burned dry, their lids fixed as if pinned open. Nothing would move, not even her lungs, as Deven recited that litany of horror. When at last she gained command of her tongue, only one word emerged. "Gunpowder?"

Gommuck shifted his weight, looking up at the Queen's consort, but Deven was staring at Magrat, his gaze suddenly unreadable. The knocker said, "Beneath the House of Lords. We found it, Scalliock and I did, when we went back to our tunnel; the storeroom we'd broken into is filled with barrels of powder. That man Fawkes is keeping watch on it."

It still didn't make sense. Deven subsided, slowly, his sword-hand falling loose once more. After a moment, he said, "You didn't know."

"I'll do as you bid me, Robin. No matter how far it goes."
"We'll be damned for it—"

Knowledge that clawed at Francis Tresham in nightmares, and put Father Garnet in an agony of indecision, contemplating the breaking of his sacred obligation. A plan that had brought death to breathe down the necks of Catholic gentleman all over London. She'd looked for it near Fawkes, and Catesby, and the rest of their circle—but not the King, nor his lords and members of Parliament.

She still could barely speak. "Lord Monteagle—"

Deven's brief exhalation was almost more a cough than a laugh. "Will preserve his own hide, no doubt. And not by staying away. He'll show that letter to Salisbury before the night is out."

Salisbury. A hideously familiar name, to anyone in the world of English Catholicism: Secretary of State to the King—which was to say his spymaster—and a devoted general for the Protestant cause. "He can't," Magrat said; her voice was working at last. "If he does—Tresham, Catesby, all the rest, they'll be *killed*. Salisbury detests Catholics; he'll do *anything* to strike at them. If Monteagle hands him my letter, and he finds out about the plot—"

"You think he doesn't already know?"

It stopped her short. Deven passed a weary hand over his brow. "He'd be a poor spymaster if this took him by surprise. But her Majesty and I have also been following the trail, and thanks to these goodly knockers we've been able to supply him— secretly— with the information he lacked."

Magrat felt suddenly like a mouse, permitted to run about because the cat knows it can't escape. There was little comfort in discovering she had other mice for company. "Then why let it go on?" she asked, unable to keep her anguish hidden. "Why not arrest them and be done with it?"

Deven looked past her and nodded; she heard the goblins back off a few steps. "To find the edges of the web," he said. "We didn't know about Tresham. Salisbury wants the whole conspiracy, down to the last man." He paused, and his expression softened into a pity that choked Magrat. "You're right that they will likely die. For the atrocity they planned, there can be no other answer. The one consolation I can offer is this: I will do what I can to make certain only the guilty are punished. Not all Catholics deserve Salisbury's hate."

She wanted to lash out at him, bury her clawed hand in his throat; she didn't want his pity, or his aid. But a memory burned within her heart, of the moment she had stepped into the tangle of this conspiracy, and the reason.

"Father Garnet," she said, addressing the hard-packed dirt of the street because it was easier than facing Deven. "He isn't part of it. He knew—but from a confession, so he couldn't tell anyone. Do you understand? He *couldn't*." No matter how terrible the secret. His duty was to God before the King.

After a moment, Deven asked, "Did he conspire with the others?"

"*No.*" His gentle soul could never have stooped to such horrors.

"Then I will do my best." Deven paused again, then said, "We are done here. I leave you with this command: *warn them not*. Any of them. For now you are free, but if you cross our work, I will not be so generous a second time."

Then his footsteps retreated down the street, followed by the two goblins. Magrat heard Gommuck mumble something that sounded like a thick Cornish apology, and then she was alone.

＊

But I will delve one yard belowe their mines,
And blowe them at the Moone.

          —William Shakespeare
          Hamlet III.iv.208-9

＊

The Tower of London: 2 May, 1606

Moving like the puppet he'd briefly become, the gaoler unlocked the door to Father Garnet's cell and let the visitor in.

Anguish and hope warred in the priest's brow when he looked up. The long months of his imprisonment had worn away at him, carving deep lines where only wrinkles had been before, but for a heartbeat something like happiness lightened his face. And Magrat, calling on every memory of every movement she'd ever seen Anne Vaux make, rushed forward to embrace him.

"My dear sister," Garnet whispered into her shoulder, the words breaking as he spoke them. "I heard you were imprisoned here, too—"

And so Mistress Vaux was, taken by force when stratagems failed to catch her. She still languished in her own cell, elsewhere in the Tower; Magrat could do nothing for her. This visit was dangerous enough, no matter what glamour disguised her, what charm held the gaoler bound.

She dug her fingers into Garnet's back. Thirty years following the man, and this was the first time she'd touched him. But she couldn't linger, however much she wanted to. "We haven't much time," she said, mimicking Anne's manner of speaking. She'd spent days practising it. "I've bribed the gaoler. Come with me, and we'll spirit you out of the Tower."

Garnet stilled, then pulled away. Then the distance between them grew: he was retreating, first one step, then another. "What?"

Magrat gritted her teeth before she could remember not to. "Freedom. In a few hours they'll come to take you to your execution; you must escape before they can."

Thirteen men lay dead already, the men who had planned the deed and tried to carry it out: Sir Everard Digby, Robert Wintour, John Grant, and Catesby's servant Thomas Bates; Tom Wintour, Ambrose Rookwood, Robert Keyes, and Guido Fawkes, all hung and drawn and quartered. Four others had escaped that fate by dying in a desperate stand at Holbeach: Jack Wright and his brother Kit, Thomas Percy, and Robin Catesby, who had brought them all to this end. Francis Tresham had screamed away the final days of his life months ago, dying of illness here in the Tower before Salisbury could put him to trial. And tomorrow, Garnet would become the fourteenth.

But this was Deven's gift to her, apology for his failure to stop Salisbury. The King's spymaster knew full well that Garnet had not planned the Gunpowder Treason, as they were calling it; but that did not matter. Garnet had *known*, and not warned anyone. And he was a Jesuit, which Salisbury hated above all else. So this man, who loved music and abhorred violence, had been painted as the architect of the plot, and would die as such.

"Why do you hesitate?" Magrat demanded, seeing Garnet retreat another step.

He stared at her, the unblinking gaze of a prey animal brought to bay. "Because you are not Anne Vaux."

It froze Magrat where she stood. Then she forced a laugh. "What? Father—"

"Who are you?" he demanded. "Did Salisbury scour all England for a woman who looked enough of a Vaux to deceive me? But why do you try to lure me away, when I am already condemned— what is there to gain? I can only be executed once."

An unbroken stream of curses flowed through Magrat's head. She shouldn't have chosen Anne—but Salisbury and his men had practised deceptions on Garnet before; the only person she could be sure of him trusting was his beloved sister in Christ. Yet that was also the one person he knew too well for her to counterfeit.

They faced off at nearly the full length of his cell, now; Garnet's back was against the wall. What could she do? Magrat thought briefly of changing her glamour—counterfeit an angel, claim she'd come to bring him salvation. The bread now protecting her meant she could speak of God as much as she wanted, without fear of destroying the illusion. But if she couldn't imitate a mortal woman well enough to persuade him, she doubted she could make a convincing angel. And the attempt alone would be an insult.

"I'm not Mistress Vaux," she blurted, as if he did not know already. "I'm sorry I lied. But I *am* here to rescue you. Please, we must go, *now*."

Garnet's jaw hardened. "Not until I know who you are."

Blood and Bone. If only she'd brought a will-o'-the-wisp to lure him. Desperate, Magrat reached for words, and found herself holding nothing but the truth.

"I'm a friend," she said quietly. "One who's followed you for years, in secret. I warned Mistress Vaux when the searchers were coming; I scared them away from your hiding-places. Hyde Abbey was once my home, but 'tis gone now, and so I've made my home with you: with the Catholics of England, and the priests who serve them. Because that's what I'm supposed to *do*. You are my church—you and your people. So I haunt you, and I know whether your dead are going to Heaven or to Hell, but I don't want to know that for you. I don't want to see your death. Please, I *beg* you, come with me, and you'll be safe."

There was still the tiniest flicker of hope. The slimmest chance, that his end might not be waiting for him with the morning's light.

His mouth had fallen open during her speech. Into the ensuing silence, Father Garnet whispered, "What are you?"

Magrat's mouth trembled, and she felt a hot pricking in her eyes. "I can't show you. My face—you'll think me evil. Just let me do this thing for you."

"Let you save me." Garnet's breath came out in a ragged, voiceless gust. "Some ancient ghost that haunts my steps, and you say you can take me from the Tower."

"Yes."

He closed his eyes, and she felt the faith gather within him, pressing against the protection that armoured her. Not an attack, a prayer to drive her back; just a fire within, giving him strength.

"No."

The word made no sense.

Garnet opened his eyes once more, and terrifying peace dwelt within them. "I could have saved myself many times before now. All I had to do was tell of Robin's plan. Salisbury, I know, does not understand, and perhaps you do not either—but an understanding came to me, when I prayed for guidance after hearing Father Tesimond's confession.

"I have long said that I trust in divine Providence to vindicate our cause here in England. We men may do all that we can, but in the end, we rise or fall by the grace of God alone. I therefore looked to my duty, and it was clear, however agonizing it might be: I could not betray Robin's sacred confidence, imparted under the seal of the confessional. I did what I could to stop him, short of breaking that seal. I thought I had succeeded. But 'twas not enough." He spread his hands, made pale and thin by his long confinement. "Thus I am here."

Magrat stared. "You'll stay and let them execute you. Because you think that is *God's will.*"

"Yes."

Frustration strangled her first attempt to answer. The second was better: "'Tis *Salisbury's* will, Father. And he's not God. You needn't let him kill you!"

"You can rescue a person from the Tower?"

"Did you not hear me say it?"

"Then rescue Anne Vaux," Garnet said. "She is blameless, and held prisoner only to strike at me. If you are the friend you claim, then do me this favour, and I will bless you to the angels, whatever unhallowed spirit you may be."

Her breath came in short, desperate gasps, as if she were trying to hold in something that threatened to break free. He *couldn't* stay—they were going to draw and quarter him—

But he'd kept silent for months, when a few words might have saved him, and other men besides. Because that was what his faith required. He would hardly abandon it now, simply to preserve his own skin. That inner fire was the only strength he had anymore.

Rescuing Anne Vaux tonight would be impossible; they'd charmed the wrong gaolers for that. But Magrat would see it done, if she had to sell herself into Deven's service forever. And one more thing, before Garnet was gone.

"I'll bring her to you in the morning," she promised, past the hardness in her throat. "In truth this time; not me in disguise. So you may see her one last time."

A broken smile found its way onto the condemned man's face. "Thank you. May the Lord bless and keep you, my friend."

His benediction broke harmlessly against the protection of mortal bread, but the words still struck something deep within.

The stone corridor outside wavered and swam in Magrat's vision as she left the cell and heard the gaoler lock the door behind her. The pricking in her eyes grew to unbearable heat, and then scalding lines tracked down her face.

No church grim should ever weep for the dead. But Magrat was a grim without a home, for the man who had given her one would be martyred tomorrow, for reasons she did not—could not—understand.

It was not duty, but choice. Alone in the harsh confines of the Tower, Magrat wept for Father Garnet.

THE DEATHS OF
CHRISTOPHER MARLOWE

THIS MUCH IS CERTAIN: that on the thirtieth day of May, in the year of our Lord 1593, events transpired in a rented room in Deptford that resulted in the corpse of a man with a knife wound in his skull, above his right eye.

In between the certainties lie a hundred tales.

"In faith," Frizer said, in the wake of a thunderous belch, "I could not eat a bite more."

The light of the late afternoon sun bathed the room in a warm glow. The three gentlemen sitting at the table had their backs to it, the better to shade their eyes, but one man lay on a bed between the table and the window, and he turned his face to the sun with a weary sigh.

The company of these gentlemen was grown tiresome to him. They had met at this house before noon, to dine together in a rented room and walk about in the garden, and here they were yet at suppertime. It was not how he would have preferred to spend his last day of liberty.

So it came as a relief when Frizer said to the two men on either side of him, "We must be on our way soon, I think, if we're to reach our destination before night." He turned in his seat to address the man on the bed. "Kit, go downstairs and settle with Widow Bull, would you? I'm too full to move."

Sitting up and brushing his hair back with one long-fingered hand, Kit said, "You mean you're too lazy to move. But if it gets us on the road, then I shan't complain. Give me your coin, and I'll pay her."

"Pay her yourself," Frizer said, with another small belch. "I am not a charitable order."

Kit flushed. The wine had gone to his head while he lay by the window, and it stoked his irritation with Frizer. "Coming here was your suggestion. Left to my own devices, I would not have spent the day here to begin with, and not in the company of these men."

The man seated to Frizer's right glared at him over one shoulder. "And what is that supposed to mean?"

"It *means*, sir, that my bail has run out, I am due to present myself once more to the Star Chamber tomorrow, and your company has hardly been so diverting as to take my mind from that matter. I will not suffer an overfed ass to demand that I pay for his day at the trough."

Frizer had his back to Kit at that moment, but it did not muffle his words enough—and perhaps the man did not mean for it to. "It's no less than you deserve, you damned atheist."

Kit surged up off the bed in a fury, lurching toward Frizer. Losing his balance, he stumbled against the other man, and his hand found the hilt of the dagger Frizer wore at his back. He snatched it loose, not thinking what he was doing; the wine he had drunk, the irritation with Frizer's penny-pinching, the fear he had lived with since his arrest by the Star Chamber, all whirled together into a rage that made him strike at Frizer with the blade.

It gouged the man's scalp, and Kit cursed his poor coordination. Frizer howled and tried to squirm free. The room was a small one, though, mostly filled with the table, the chairs, and the bed, and with the other two men on either side of him he had nowhere to go. Kit struck a second time, cutting Frizer's scalp once more, and then lost his balance again as his target turned and began to struggle with him over the knife.

The man who holds a dagger's hilt has the advantage, but Kit had disadvantages besides. He was drunk; he was weary; he was half Frizer's size. And then the backs of his knees hit the bed and he fell, Frizer on top of him.

The dagger stabbed into the bone above his right eye.

Ingram Frizer swore and stumbled back to his feet, staring at what he had wrought. Blood spread silently outward from the body on the bed.

Christopher Marlowe, poet and dramatist of the English stage, was dead.

And so that the said Ingram killed & slew Christopher Morley…in the defence and saving of his own life against our peace our crown & dignity. As more fully appears by the tenor of the Record of the Inquisition aforesaid which we caused to come before us in our Chancery by virtue of our writ. We therefore moved by piety have pardoned the same Ingram ffrisar the breach of our peace which pertains to us against the said Ingram for the death above mentioned & grant to him our firm peace….

—pardon issued by Elizabeth, by the Grace of God,
Queen of England, France and Ireland,
Defender of the Faith &c,
28th day of June, anno Domini 1593

This much is known of Christopher Marlowe.

He was a shoemaker's son from Canterbury who attended the college of Corpus Christi in Cambridge, where he achieved the degree of Bachelor of Arts. Several years later this became a Master's degree, after the Queen's Privy Council intervened to quash a rumour of his conversion to Catholicism. He wrote approximately half a dozen plays, several poems, and translations of Latin works, and made great advances in the dramatic use of blank verse.

On the twentieth day of May, in the year of our Lord 1593, he was arrested on a charge of atheism, then released for a short time on bail.

"In faith," Frizer said, in the wake of a thunderous belch, "I could not eat a bite more."

The light of the late afternoon sun bathed the room in a warm glow. The three gentlemen sitting at the table had their backs to it, the better to shade their eyes, but one man lay on a bed between the table and the window, and he turned his face to the sun with an irritated sigh.

Poley ignored Frizer's excess. Instead he said over his shoulder to the man on the bed, "Your odds don't look very good, Master Marlowe."

"Atheism and blasphemy," Kit said in a dismissive tone. "Kyd's words against me won't amount to much. And Baines was defecting to the Catholics when we lived in Flushing together— why do you think Burghley let me go? He knew *I* wasn't the defector, whatever Baines said. But the evidence against Baines was lacking, and so he's free to fabricate these new accusations against me. Now I'm an atheist, when last year I was a Catholic in the making?"

Skeres said, from the other side of Frizer, "You're fortunate it's just atheism. The original version of Baines' accusation included sedition as well."

"Henry Barrow and John Greenwood were hanged for that scarcely a month gone," Poley added, hard on the heels of Skeres' ominous words. "And John Penry just yesterday."

Kit's head had come up when Skeres mentioned sedition, but now he lay back with a wave of one hand. "There is no proof."

"Proof is not needed," Skeres said. "Only confession."

"Confession such as was extracted from your friend Kyd," Poley said. "And you are no more immune to the rack than he,

Master Marlowe."

The two of them passed their words back and forth as smoothly as if they'd rehearsed in advance. Frizer remained silent, his back to Kit, his shoulders hunched as if uncomfortable with the entire situation. The four of them had been at it all day. The conversation periodically diverged to other topics as they walked in the garden during the afternoon hours, but always it returned to this: the threat against Kit.

Kit sat up and draped his arms over his knees, long-fingered hands hanging loose. "Confession and recantation. Unpleasant, but I'd hardly be the first man to escape execution thus."

Poley looked at him with cold, hard eyes that would not have been out of place in a wolf's head. "Master Marlowe, I do not believe you understand the true gravity of the situation.

"No one is alone in this matter. An Arianist tract was found in Thomas Kyd's room, which he claims you gave to him. You have not said whether this is true or not, but in the final accounting it does not matter. *You were named.* And you, in your turn, will name others."

No man among them was reckless enough to speak the names aloud, but they whispered through Kit's mind. Henry Percy, called the "Wizard" Earl of Northumberland. Sir George Carey, heir to the Lord Chamberlain. Ferdinando Stanley, Lord Strange. Sir Walter Ralegh, disgraced at Court, but not so disgraced that he could not fall yet further.

Kit had not been so foolish as to print his thoughts on atheism—but he had, it was true, spoken of them to those men, who lent him a sympathetic ear. And atheism was as good as sedition, when the Queen was the head of the Church and ruled in God's name.

Powerful men, every one of them, who would not stand by to see their names dragged into this incident.

"Or rather," Poley said, continuing where he had left off and interrupting Kit's suddenly ominous thoughts, "you will *not* name others. We are to see to that."

And Frizer rose at last, his face grim but set, drawing from the small of his back a dagger which had rested there all this time—a dagger which Kit might have seized, had he thought more quickly, but the wine blinded him to his peril until too late. He screamed and lunged off the bed, hoping against all reason that the Widow Bull might hear and somehow intervene, but Skeres and Poley grabbed his arms and threw him back onto the bed, and Frizer stabbed downward with the knife.

Kit's flailing meant Frizer missed his mark, but the blade did its work regardless, sinking into the bone above his right eye.

The three men stood up, breathing hard in the aftermath of the brief struggle. Blood spread silently outward from the body on the bed.

"Give me your dagger," Poley said to his companion Frizer. "I'll cut your scalp, and we shall say he attacked you."

They did so, and then went for the Widow Bull, to report the terrible news.

Christopher Marlowe, atheist and threat to those more powerful than he, was dead.

These thinges, with many other shall by good & honest witnes be aproved to be his opinions and Comon Speeches, and that this Marlow doth not only hould them himself, but almost into every Company he Cometh he perswades men to Atheism willing them not to be afeard of bugbeares and hobgoblins, and vtterly scorning both god and his ministers as I Richard Baines will Justify & approue both by mine oth and the testimony of many honest men, and almost al men with whome he hath Conversed any time will testify the same, and as I think all men in Cristianity ought to indevor that the mouth of so dangerous a member may be stopped....

—*statement of accusation by Richard Baines*

This much is known of the persons involved.

Ingram Frizer was a servant and agent of Thomas Walsingham. Less famous than his cousin, Sir Francis Walsingham, who had late been Secretary of State to Her Majesty Queen Elizabeth, Thomas was nonetheless in the same business as that recently-deceased cousin: the business of espionage.

Nicholas Skeres served Sir Francis as an "agent provocateur" in the matter of the Babington Plot against the Queen's life, and had assisted Frizer in conning a naive young man out of his money. Robert Poley, even more than Skeres and Frizer, had experience as Sir Francis' spy. On that day in Deptford, he was carrying political letters from the Netherlands to the Court, currently in residence twelve miles away at the Palace of Nonsuch.

The house belonged to one Dame Eleanor Bull. She was a respectable widow whose sister had connections to the Court, and she often hired out her rooms for meetings, serving meals to those who came there.

That she provided a safe house for the Government's spies is purely speculation.

As for Christopher Marlowe, he had done "good service" to Her Majesty—earning the assistance of the Privy Council, when he would have been denied his degree—and his artistic patron was the gentleman Thomas Walsingham.

"In faith," Frizer said, in the wake of a thunderous belch, "I could not eat a bite more."

The light of the late afternoon sun bathed the room in a warm glow. The three gentlemen sitting at the table had their backs to it, the better to shade their eyes, but one man lay on a bed between the table and the window, and he turned his face to the sun with a worried sigh.

A knock at the door brought everyone alert, even Frizer, who had been relaxed the entire day, in contrast to his companions' tension. Skeres rose and went to the door, cracking it just a sliver.

Muffled but still intelligible, the Widow Bull's voice said, "They're here."

Skeres glanced back at Frizer and jerked his head. "Come help me."

When the two men had left the room, the last gentleman at the table turned in his seat to look at the bed. "Are you ready, Kit?"

The fine-boned face was drawn and weary. Kit had not rested well these days past, since Thomas Kyd issued his accusation from the rack, since word came that Baines was preparing worse troubles for him. Atheism, potentially sedition; men accused of these things did not fare well.

"I imagine the rack would be more painful," he said by way of response to Poley, "but at the moment, it is hard to credit."

Whatever Poley might have said to that was forestalled by the return of Frizer and Skeres, dragging a heavy, wrapped bundle through the door. Kit rolled smoothly to his feet as Poley went to pull the sheets from one end of the bundle.

"God's blood!" Kit swore when the wrappings came free, revealing the face of a dead man. "Who is that?"

"John Penry," Poley said. "Or should I say, Kit Marlowe."

Kit sank back against the table, eyes still on the corpse. The man was dark-haired, fairly slender. Not a close resemblance, as such things went, but close enough for Poley's words to make his skin crawl. "You mean not just to spirit me from England. You mean to fake my death."

"Of course." Poley stepped aside as Frizer and Skeres, panting from the effort of carrying the body up the stairs, began to extract it from its wrappings. "The forces moving against you would not be satisfied if you merely disappeared. Alive, Kit Marlowe is still a threat, and a potential source of evidence against powerful men. Dead, no one will think on him again."

Poley's blunt words staggered Kit. He gripped the edges of the table to keep himself steady. The rack would be more painful, yes—he kept that well in mind. But he did not wish to be forgotten. He would almost dare imprisonment and execution, rather than the world's disregard.

"This isn't going to work," he said desperately, as Penry's body rolled clear of the winding sheet. "He's been dead for some time."

"One day." Skeres paused to brush his hair clear of his eyes. "Hanged at St. Thomas-a-Watering yesterday—for sedition, as it happens. Look upon your potential fate, Master Marlowe."

Kit ignored the jibe. "Yes, exactly. *Hanged.*" He gestured at the livid bruising around Penry's neck. "What are you doing to do, say I accidentally strangled myself in the bedsheets?"

As if to say yes, Frizer and Skeres began to manoeuver the corpse onto the bed. Poley said, "It's taken care of. We're within the verge; the Queen is at Nonsuch still. That means the Coroner of the Queen's Household must be involved, and we have secured Danby's assistance. How do you think we obtained Penry's body? Danby will keep the county coroner out of it, and ensure no one examines the body too closely."

Secured Danby's assistance. For the first time, Kit began to appreciate just how far the conspiracy to save his life stretched. Was the Queen herself involved? He would never be fool enough to ask, nor arrogant enough to assume it.

But he knew full well that, in the final accounting, this had little to do with saving his life. Even his patron, Thomas Walsingham, would not go to such lengths merely to preserve one scribbler of poetry. All of this was happening because of the threat to men more powerful than he. His survival was a gift, in remembrance of the services he had done Her Majesty's government.

A gift he would not spurn, though its price wounded his heart. And, in truth, his pride.

"Your clothes, Master Marlowe," Poley said, and setting his jaw to hide the pain he felt, Kit began to strip. Skeres and Frizer wrestled the corpse into his garments, while he put on those Poley provided.

When the dressing was done, Frizer drew his dagger and looked at Poley uncertainly.

"The face," Poley said. "On Danby's orders. He can show the

face to be identified and examined, without showing the throat."

Frizer looked ill, but turned back to the body on the bed. He leaned over, dagger in hand, set the point against Penry's dead skin, and thrust.

Kit, watching this happen, gave a bark of disbelieving laughter. "You cretin—you might have stabbed him in the *eye*, at least. But *above* the eye? That wouldn't even kill a man, not right away, not a wound that shallow. You—"

"Do it yourself, if you're so eager to aid," Frizer snarled, shoving the blade in Kit's general direction.

Poley intercepted it, taking the weapon from Frizer's hand. "Skeres, there's a jug of pig's blood in the corner. Pour it onto the face and the sheets. Frizer, hold still. It needs to look like he attacked you. We'll say there was an argument over the bill." Without waiting for a response, he struck Frizer twice over the head with the dagger, cutting his scalp, causing the man to yelp in sudden anger.

Kit had sagged down into one of the chairs as his companions went about faking his death with callous efficiency. John Penry now had his clothes, his name. Blood spread silently outward from the body on the bed.

Christopher Marlowe, poet, atheist, and agent to Her Majesty's government, was dead.

Or so the world must believe.

...& after supper the said Ingram & Christopher Morley were in speech & uttered one to the other divers malicious words for the reason that they could not be at one nor agree about the payment of the sum of pence, that is, le recknynge, there; & the said Christoper Morley was then lying upon a bed in the room where they supped, & moved with anger against the said Ingram Frizer upon the words as spoken between them [...] in which affray the same Ingram could not get away from the said Christopher Morley; and so it befell in

the affray that the said Ingram, in defence of his life, with the dagger aforesaid of the value of 12d. gave the said Christopher then & there a mortal wound over his right eye of the depth of two inches & the width of one inch; of which mortal wound the aforesaid Christopher Morley then & there instantly died...

> *—statement of inquest issued by William Danby,*
> *Coroner of the Queen's Household,*
> *1st day of June, anno Domini 1593*

✳

Kit Marlowe died at the hands of one Ingram Frizer, in an argument over the bill.

Perhaps.

He was murdered at the behest of Sir Walter Ralegh; of Robert Devereux, the Earl of Essex; of William Cecil, Lord Burghley, and his son Sir Robert Cecil. He was murdered on the orders of the Lord Admiral and the Lord Chamberlain; of Audrey Walsingham, Thomas' wife; of Queen Elizabeth herself.

Perhaps.

He did not die at all, but went overseas, and returned two years later under the name Le Doux. He wrote the plays of William Shakespeare, because his pride could not allow him to abandon poetry.

Perhaps. Or perhaps not.

He vanished from history's page, and for a man of his temperament, perhaps that was no different from death.

As the sun set on the thirtieth day of May, in the year of our Lord 1593, a man lay on a bed in Deptford, with a knife wound in the bone above his right eye. Twelve men witnessed the body, under the direction of the queen's coroner, and swore their oaths upon the matter.

That much is certain—no more.

TWO PRETENDERS

HE SPENDS HIS DAYS sitting at the window, like a maiden in some troubadour's tale. Watching the life of the fortress go by. The King is not in residence; the King, perhaps, does not want daily reminders of the prisoners who share his palace. Out from under the royal eye, the servants and soldiers move at a gentler pace, exchanging jokes in the courtyard, or resting for a moment in the warmth of summer's sun.

After a year of watching them, he is bored enough to fling himself to the paving-stones below—if only the window were large enough. And if only the shackles did not hold him back.

The alternative to boredom is remembrance. And that, he avoids at all costs.

A creak, as the door opens behind him. The prisoner does not bother to turn around. His dinner doesn't interest him—and if it isn't his dinner, if it's some minion of the King come to knife him in the back, well, there's no particular merit in being knifed in the front instead. He hears the expected clack of a bowl set upon the floor, and waits…but the door does not creak closed.

Nor does a blade free him from this Purgatory. No, that sort of work happens in the dead of night. That is when the would-be murderer comes to—

The prisoner jerks, as if to throw off the memory by force. *Not a memory. A dream. A mad fancy, and not a good one, at that.*

Turning shows him the scene behind: the bowl on the floor, and the open door. But the young man standing a few steps inside his cell isn't the usual guard. Something about him is familiar, and so the prisoner stops, very suddenly, staring at his face.

"Forgive me for disturbing you," the young man says. The words come out by rote: whatever occupies his mind, it isn't apology. "Are—are you Perkin Warbeck?"

Hysterical laughter rises up in the prisoner's throat like vomit, and is choked down the same way. To be asked that, *now*, on the heels of insistent memory, and this young man's face like an echo—

"They tell me I am," he says, before he can think better of it. Of course he's Perkin Warbeck. So his parents called him, and his life depends upon his agreement.

His life. Such as it is.

The young man says, "I brought you your food."

Any man with eyes could see that. More rote words, as if this stranger is delaying—either his departure from the room, or his real purpose in coming. Warbeck merely waits, until the young man shifts uncomfortably and looks at the battered shoes on his feet. Then Warbeck asks, "Did you come to stare? See the pretender to England's crown, only a farthing a look, but if you want to throw anything you'll have to pay more—"

"No!" His cell is small; the young man's denial rings sharply off the stone. "No," he repeats, more softly. "I—I was once a prisoner here, too. I know how tedious it becomes. I wanted to offer my sympathy."

Against his will, curiosity pricks through the apathy in which Warbeck has wrapped himself. The Tower of London is no place for ordinary captives. This is where the King keeps nobles, traitors—

—his kin—

He shoves the thought back again.

There's something odd about the stranger's face. A young man, yes, but *how* young? It's difficult to say. Warbeck thought the fellow a few years his own junior; now he is not so sure. He might even be older. And familiar...yes, the look is there. The Yorkist look, calling to mind the long wars between the House of York and the House of Lancaster, before Henry Tudor came to settle them all, by marriage and the sword.

With that understanding comes a name. "You're Lambert Simnel."

The visitor ducks his head again. Warbeck fights down another urge to laugh. Two pretenders, meeting face-to-face at last. He takes some pride in the fact that his own rebellion got further; on the other hand, Simnel was crowned in Dublin, which was more than Warbeck ever achieved. Edward VI, they'd called that false King, because he was supposed to be the young Earl of Warwick. Cousin to the dethroned boy-King Edward V, who along with his brother the Duke of York was murdered—so they said—by King Richard. Here in this very Tower. A sordid and useful tale, for those who opposed Richard. Like Henry Tudor, who had succeeded him.

Warbeck has seen the young earl. Another prisoner, just like him, just like the murdered boy-King and his brother. Simnel's supporters claimed *that* earl was the impostor, of course. The resemblance is a good one, allowing for the fact that Warwick is a simpleton, and Lambert Simnel is not. There's intelligence behind those eyes, though it seems he's learned to cast them down with a servant's proper humility.

"Tell me, Simnel," Warbeck says, lifting one of his shackles, "do you envy me? I may be chained here, but you're chained to the spits in the King's kitchen. His mercy to you may be worse than his cruelty to me."

Simnel smiles faintly, unreadably. "King Henry understood that I was a mere boy, the puppet of those around me, and not to be blamed for their treason."

A mere boy. Warbeck heard from one man that Simnel was ten at the time of the rebellion; another said he was sixteen. Seeing him now, Warbeck understands the confusion. Time grips every man the same—but not this one.

Simnel moves at last, easing the door almost shut before coming further into the room. The state of the door hardly matters. Warbeck is chained, and even if he weren't, there are guards between him and the stairs; and beyond them, the royal palace and fortress of the Tower of London. There will be no impromptu escapes, whether Simnel closes the door or not.

So Warbeck merely shifts aside, allowing his visitor access to the narrow slit of the window. It's a novelty, having companionship in his cell. He tries not to think about how it will feel when Simnel goes away and he is left here, alone once more, with nothing but false memories to occupy him.

The young man closes his eyes, appreciating the cool breeze across his face. It's a look Warbeck recognises: the attitude of the prisoner, slipping briefly into the dream of freedom. Yes, Simnel knows how it feels, as only a fellow captive can.

But the King granted him mercy. When was he ever here?

Before he can decide whether to ask or not, Simnel poses his own question. "What do you think he intends to do with you?"

Henry Tudor. The new King, as Warbeck keeps thinking of him, even though he's been on the throne nearly fourteen years. Many people talk that way. There are men of forty who don't remember a time when England's crown was secure. Four usurpations, one King cut down in battle, and one dead either peacefully or by poison, depending on who tells the story. And more than a few rebellions. If Henry feels uncertain about the stability of his rule, no one can blame him.

"If I'm lucky? He'll keep me here," Warbeck says. "The value of displaying me on his progresses has declined, and then I escaped once, so now he *knows* he can't trust me." That escape still makes Warbeck's mind itch, like grit in a shoe. Wondering if Henry let it happen. As an excuse to confine him more harshly.

Or because he believes the stories. But that would mean that Henry, too, is mad, just like one Perkin Warbeck.

It's Simnel's face that makes him think these things, bringing the memories up like water from a buried spring. Turning his mind to mud. Warbeck faces the room instead, going to the limit of his chains. "And there's only one end for those a King cannot trust."

"I won't let him hurt you."

The declaration hovers in the air, like an arrow in mid-flight. The instinctive answer of a protector—as if Simnel really were the elder of the two, and sheltering Warbeck against the shadow of the headsman's axe. Warbeck has just a moment to anticipate the pain; then the arrow strikes home.

I won't let him hurt you. Words he's heard before—his memory insists upon it, against the evidence of his reason. Not just the words, but the place, the voice, the fear of death; the dam has broken, and all the things he dares not think of, all the things that cannot be, come flooding back to drown him.

He swore never to speak of it, not to anyone, but his tongue betrays him in an instant. Staring blindly into the dark corner of his cell, he murmurs, "Sometimes I think I've been here before. In my dreams...I have the strangest dreams."

He pauses, fighting not to say more, and into that pause comes the young man's quiet answer. "Dreams of this place. Not this cell—a proper chamber, with a proper bed, and servants, and no shackles. But a prison just the same."

"And a cruel King. Like in the stories your nursemaid tells. He steals the crown, and locks away the two boys who stand in his path—"

"The boy-King of England," the young man says, "and his little brother, a royal Duke."

Slowly—more slowly than the roasting spits in the King's kitchen—the prisoner turns back. The light through the window gilds one side of the young man's face, and now his age truly is impossible to guess, but the prisoner knows. The one they call Lambert Simnel is older than he, however little it appears to be so.

And they share the same memories.

Strange enough memories, for two men like them, to think they've been here before. But that is the easy part, the *sane* part. He could have lived with such dreams, and scarcely been troubled. What comes next is such madness that he has buried it for fifteen years, so deeply it can only be uncovered by nightmares.

The man who is not Simnel smiles, without humour. "The tale goes on, doesn't it? The children are afraid, so very afraid, that their uncle will murder them, in order to protect the crown he has taken. But a beautiful lady finds them, and soothes away their fright."

Her face is indistinct, after all these years spent convincing himself it was never real. Perhaps she was beautiful; perhaps not. Her gentle voice, though, whispers in his mind, as if she stood even now at his shoulder. *Hush, little one; there is nothing to fear so long as you are with me....*

He remembers her promise all too well. And a boy trying to be a man, saying, *I won't let him hurt you.*

All of it so very like a tale. "The boy-King begs her to protect them. And late one night, when their uncle comes their chamber—"

The creak of the door; shoes touching down with exquisite care upon the floor, as if afraid of waking the stone itself. A muffled whimper: neither boy is asleep, and the little Duke is trying so hard not to cry. He mustn't be a child now; his brother has asked him to be strong. They have to be strong, because Mother isn't here, and neither is the lady who swore she would watch over them. But he is so afraid....

Then comes her voice, singing like the sun itself, until the chamber somehow glows without light. A voice that speaks of dainty sweets, and meadows in which to play, and lullabies when bedtime comes; of safety and warmth and freedom from care. His throat aches with sudden yearning. To be there—oh, to be *there* and not here, to go far, far away—

What must it have looked like, to his uncle and the knight who accompanied him? Did they see the boys go, see the creature that took them? He doesn't know. All he knows is this: one moment he was in that dark chamber, fearing his own death; the next, they both were with the lady, who promised they would never want for anything again.

It wasn't true. Safety and warmth and freedom from care—what they had was a child's dream of such things, and once a boy tries to be a man, he can't go back. The little Duke might have accepted it, but his brother, older and wiser, would not let him. And so that paradise was broken.

He whispers, "I got lost on the way back. I ended up in

France."

Regret shadows his brother's face, showing the greater age he rightfully claims, and more besides. "Better that than staying...I was there three years, I think. It was three years here, at least. You see what it did to me. At times it was like she promised, but the rest...."

He doesn't have to explain. That adults might promise one thing but deliver another was a lesson these two learned at an early age.

A journey out of wonder, that ended with him stumbling down a narrow street in a town he later learned was Tournai. A couple who adopted him, and gave him a new name, because he could not remember his own; that was one of the things he lost on the way back, paying it to some hideous creature as fee for his passage. A new life, wherein he learned not to think about the things he did remember, until the day he went to Ireland and saw coins bearing a face he recognised. A face he had once called *Father*. It had that look, the Yorkist look, and so did he; a few gentlemen saw that and decided to make use of it. They never knew—because he did not tell them—the terrible irony in their decision to declare him Richard, the long-lost Duke of York.

As if he hears that thought, the young man by the window smiles. Painfully. "I did not look old enough to be King Edward," he says. "The three years I lost...over there. So they proclaimed me a different Edward instead. It was almost the same."

The simpleton Earl of Warwick, locked away in the same prison they had escaped. Their tale fell apart in the end; the evil uncle did not die at the hand of the boy-King, returned in triumph from his flight out of this mortal world. Richard III fell instead at Bosworth, fighting another usurper. And by the time the lost young Edward came back, by the time the lost young Richard remembered his name, it was too late; that usurper was Henry VII, the first Tudor King, and the crown rested firmly on his head.

They had tried anyway. Both of them had. And this is where it left them: the boy-King turning spits of meat in Henry's kitchens, and the little Duke once more in the Tower.

If this is the madness of Perkin Warbeck, at least he can take comfort in knowing that Lambert Simnel shares it, too.

I won't let him hurt you.

A declaration that never changes, no matter what has passed. His brother nods once, a swift movement, as if someone could be watching through the high, narrow window. "I can try," he whispers. "You and Ned. But it will be dangerous."

Escape. Maybe another rebellion. Coronation, either for him or Ned, Edward of Warwick, their poor simple cousin. Or perhaps for one Lambert Simnel, who looks enough like Ned to pass—so long as Henry cannot prove the lie by showing the earl in his possession.

For nearly forty years, men have torn at the crown of England like dogs fighting over a bone. Yorkists and Lancasters and a Tudor to bring the houses together, and much good has all that fighting done anyone. But his alternative is this: a cell, and chains, and the possibility of execution anyway. Right back where he began, but in less comfort. And this time there is no lady with a beautiful voice to offer him the dream of safety.

He wouldn't accept if she did. His brother is the only one he can trust.

A brief, fierce embrace, away from the window's gaze; the two cling to each other now not like boys but men, reunited after years and worlds apart. For all the rumours, all the stories of how Richard III murdered the princes in the Tower, and even their supposed impostures and bids for the throne, nothing comes close to the truth—and nothing ever will. Only with each other can they be honest, in this fleeting moment of reunion.

It cannot last. The servant has stayed too long already; the guards will wonder what he is doing. They hold onto it as long as they can, Richard, Duke of York, and the deposed King Edward V of England; then they step apart and are Perkin Warbeck and Lambert Simnel once more.

Pretenders indeed. But not in the way that King Henry believes.

When the door is closed, and he is alone in the cell, he goes back to his seat at the window. But this time, he does not watch the servants and soldiers as they go about their work.

This time—for the first time in fifteen years—he permits himself to remember.

THE DAMNATION OF
ST. TERESA OF ÁVILA

THEY WERE ON THE ROAD from Burgos to Alba de Tormes when she fell ill. The men who escorted her were careful not to mutter where she could hear; they knew she would chide them for it. She had suffered worse than the rain which poured down on them unceasing, worse than an archbishop who summoned an old woman miles across Spain and then turned her away. She had endured excommunication, the Inquisition, and sixty-seven years of life. This was merely the latest and least of her trials.

But they did mutter where she could not hear. They were not as holy as she, not as generous of spirit. They resented her ill-treatment when it was merely an insult; when her brow heated and she began to cough, they did more than resent it. In low voices they blamed the archbishop, the noblewoman who called for the most revered of nuns to attend her in childbed. The infant was already born when they arrived; once again, she had been brought all this way for nothing.

Not for nothing: that was what she would have said, if she knew of their complaints. God brought her here for a purpose.

God brought her here to die.

She was too ill to be moved, burning up with fever. By the night of October 4th, they knew her end was near. Her last words, whispered to her confessor, were: "My Lord, it is time to move on. Well then, may your will be done. O my Lord and my Spouse, the hour that I have longed for has come. It is time to meet one another."

She was dead come the following morning: October 15th,

anno Domini 1582.

The night of her death lasted for ten days.

Not since the great illness of her youth has she known such suffering.

Fever permeates her body like a stain, seeping into every fibre of her being. She cannot move her limbs without pain, cannot swallow without agony, cannot even draw breath without that gentle movement jarring her head and making her vision swim. Lying prostrate in her narrow bed, she floats on a sea of fire. The recollection comes to her dimly of a holy man she had admired very much—she cannot recollect his name through the haze—whose response to great cold was to take off his cloak and open the door and window of his tiny cell. He did this, he told her, so that his body might enjoy the meagre increase of warmth when he closed the portals once more. She would emulate him if she could, but she cannot think how she might increase the heat from which she suffers. Perhaps there is a fireplace in the room?

It is foolish of her to lie in bed thus, and so to neglect her duties to God. Has she not learned again and again the futility of giving comfort to her body? She has never fared better than when she ignored her physical well-being and turned her thoughts only to the Sacred Humanity, whose suffering was so much greater than her own.

Despite her resolution to bear this cross with fortitude, a cry escapes her lips when she rolls over in her bed. Her arms shake like reeds in the wind as she tries to push herself upright: tries, and fails. Instead she slips her legs over the edge of the bed and slides until her knees strike the stone below. She cannot rise to look for a fireplace, for wood to burn and increase the heat, but this will do. There by the bed she does not need—his name was Peter of Alcantara, she remembers, and he slept upright with his head pillowed on a beam of wood—she kneels and folds her hands in prayer. Her body settles into this accustomed position with the familiarity of decades. She will not fall, unless God sees fit to grace her with His transformative presence. And that is not a thing she can bring about of her own effort or will. She must wait in humility, and turn her thoughts to Heaven.

For a day and a night she prays, her body shaking with the fire of lethal fever, wracked by torment she embraces with joy.

On the second day a servant comes to her, bearing food and drink. The woman exclaims in distress to see the nun out of bed, kneeling in obedience to God, and urges her to rest. "The Lord cannot doubt your devotion, after so many years," she says, trying to lift the dying woman from her place on the unforgiving stone.

The nun laughs at her. It is a thin, reedy sound, her voice worn almost to nothing by the fever. "Oh no, my child. It is a wonder that God should bestow any graces at all upon one so wicked as I. Time and time again He has shown me His favour, and time and time again I have turned away from it to dissipate myself in trivial pastimes. I have met many who are more deserving of such gifts than I am. How can I spurn Him again, when His generosity is so boundless?"

"You are not wicked," the serving-woman says. "You are the holiest nun in Spain. Even the greatest men of the Church acknowledge your worthiness."

"I have committed many sins for which I deserve hell. It is no credit to me that anyone should think well of me, for it means only that I have deceived them by hiding my great wickedness—which is another act for which I should repent."

The serving-woman stares at her in disbelief. "It is not so! There are wicked men and women in the world, but you are not counted among them. You do no justice to yourself, nor to any other, by weighing your own sins so heavily."

She cannot be made to rise from her knees. The serving-woman instead nods to the tray laid on a table and says, "Will you not at least take sustenance? You must fortify yourself, for the road ahead is long, and you must walk to its end."

But the nun smiles at her and says, "I would do better to feast upon the stale bread and bitter herbs of my own faults, than to feed myself in luxury. Peter of Alcantara ate but once every three days; it was very easy, he said, for those who accustom themselves to it."

And upon her words there is a bowl in her hands, filled with the rankest foul matter. From this she eats, choking on every bite, and then returns to her prayer.

On the third day she attains a measure of grace: the prayer of quiet.

In this state she is still capable of thought, and so she chides herself for conceiving of the moment as an achievement. She has achieved nothing. She is capable of nothing. Her actions are as nothing compared with the power of the Lord. Though she labours with great effort to bring her spirit closer to God, she cannot do one hundredth as well as her beloved Father in Heaven, without whom nothing is possible.

The prayer of quiet does not free her from the awareness of her dying body. The pain in her knees is excruciating, from hours pressed against the unforgiving stone. She trembles in every limb, caught between the heat of fever and the chill of the air, and sweat pours down her body to soak her robes. But she welcomes her suffering with open arms, knowing it is a gift from God. He is present with her now, separate but at her side, as a friend might sit nearby in silent companionship.

How much better is this, O Lord, than the worthless friend-ships with which she filled her youth! Once she squandered much of her time and thought on frivolous matters, which in those days seemed a source of pleasure to her, for she had no awareness of their cost to her soul. Now she knows those things, which once seemed so sweet, are poison compared to this: to sit in company with God, her thoughts bent wholly to sacred matters.

If His Majesty is merciful and kind, He will carry her yet further before He is done.

Even partial union with the divine cannot last forever. The next day she is alone once more, and grieves for the loss of holy companionship. When the door opens she turns away from it, not wishing to speak with the serving-woman again. She misses the solitude and silence of the cloister, which she laboured for many years to restore after it fell into worldliness and distraction.

But the voice that comes from behind her is too deep for a woman—and familiar, though she has not heard it for many a year.

"My daughter."

There is grief in his voice, and love. Her thoughts should be bent entirely upon God, but against her better judgment she turns to look. In the doorway stands her father, in the prime of his life, younger than she is now. Sorrow lines his mouth and eyes as he looks upon her, weakened, dying.

The sight shakes her to the bone. "Father," she whispers, with lips cracked and bleeding from the dryness of the air. "Why are you here?"

He kneels with her, takes her trembling hands in his. Strong palms, broad, in which her own skeletal fingers look as fragile as winter twigs. "My poor daughter," he says, full of compassion. "Only you, in all the world, are caught in such a manner."

She wraps her fingers around the edges of his hands. The impulse is in her to take strength from his presence; she shakes it off. "What do you mean?"

"In your dying moments you turned your thoughts to God, and so you are caught outside of time. In the world from which you are departing, a great change is occurring. The drift of days and years have taken Easter from its proper place in the seasons, and so by command of His Holiness, Pope Gregory XIII, the calendar must be put right. Ten days shall never be—except for you.

"My daughter, you are transfixed upon the point of death; and there you must remain until those days have run their course."

She can see the tears lining his eyes, shining gold in the light of the fire that never needs tending. "It grieves me to see you afflicted thus."

She shakes her head, and the world dances like a mirage. "I have neither need nor wish to accept your grief. Often have I bent my thoughts to the agony of our Saviour upon the Cross, the scourging which preceded it. I have mortified my own flesh so as to share in His suffering, bloodying myself with a lash upon my own back. But for many years now I have felt as if I lived in a dream, taking little sense of pleasure or pain from anything which may happen to me. It is a great joy to be permitted to feel this torment."

Her words wrack her father. He releases her hands and reaches as if to embrace her, but she spurns it with an upraised hand. He says, "This torment may be inevitable, but it is not a thing in which to rejoice."

"How can it not be?" Her smile is beatific. "It is a gift from His Majesty, who plunges me into the depths of suffering so I may better know His love."

Her father shakes his head. "My daughter, my daughter…that is not the love of the Lord."

"I know no other," she says, and returns to her prayer.

On the following day, she enters a state of ecstasy, the second stage of prayer.

Her soul is swept up in familiar bonds, to which she submits with joy. Who would refuse to be the prisoner of Him whom she loves? Her limbs are no longer hers to move, and memory fades in the face of the overwhelming presence of God. She could, by great effort, bestir herself from this glorious union; she could direct her thoughts to her worthless flesh, cease her prayer and rise from her knees. But why would she? Nothing she could do in life or in the lingering moment of her death would equal the merit of this experience. And so she remains, transfixed like a moth upon a pin of red-hot iron.

There was a time when she refused this state. Her confessors feared it was a delusion sent by Satan, not a gift from God, and so they urged her away from it. The more they urged, the more frequently it came upon her, in defiance not only of their orders but of her own desire to bend to their will. Now there is none to obey but the Lord, and she is helpless before His might. Tears stream down her face, a waterfall without end, as she relinquishes all to His Majesty. In the depths of her soul she wishes for more, and despises herself for that wish, for she knows she is not worthy even of so much as this.

This sin, like all the others, she lays before God, and knows she does not deserve His forgiveness.

When the priest enters the next day, she wants to curse him, for upon his arrival her ecstasy ends.

"My child," he says, and his words recall her to herself. They echo her earthly father, as this man is her spiritual; she does not remember her father leaving. But only the two of them, nun and priest, are in the room now. "We must speak."

To him she does owe obedience, and so she struggles to rise. Her legs will not support her; spikes of pain thrust up through her body when she tries, so great she cannot even cry out. The priest aids her, lifting her to her feet and holding her there as her knees slowly grind straight.

"Your piety does you great credit," he says, "but you need not carry it so far. Our Father in Heaven is merciful and forgiving. He does not demand devotion beyond human endurance."

Her voice is thin and gasping, a mere ghost of itself. "I will endure any pain in His name."

"But you need not do so." He lowers her to the edge of the bed, but she will not lie down when he urges. "My child, it is no sin to rest. Your suffering will soon be done."

"I pray it is not so." Whether the sounds that comes from her mouth is a laugh or a sob, even she could not say. "When I am without His presence, I am dead; only in suffering for Him do I live."

The priest's face becomes stern. "You speak of things you do not truly understand. I tell you that you are in error, and you argue?"

She turns her face to the wall. "I have had confessors—I will not name them—who assured me that certain actions were no sin at all, when I know them to be venial, and that others were venial sins which are more rightly judged mortal. I am obedient to my spiritual director, even when he tells me to spurn God's presence, to spit upon Jesus when he comes; I have done this knowing that God will forgive me, for my obedience is correct, even if the direction I have received is wrong. But you are not my spiritual director."

"But what," he says, "if you have been advised wrongly again? St. Ignatius feared he had sinned when he trod upon two sticks of straw that had fallen in the shape of a cross. He saw in time that this was mere scrupulosity, not a true awareness of sin. What if God is not so strict as you believe, His judgment not so harsh?"

She bows her head, clasps her hands in her lap. "I have no power to confront my sin, no ability to overcome it. Only His Majesty can do so. All I may hope for is to subject myself utterly to His will, and pray."

The priest is gone. Biting down on a whimper, she leaves her bed to kneel upon the stone once more.

The memory comes to her that she wrote once of a moment much like this. In describing the third degree of prayer, the experience of ecstatic union, she said it was "like a dying man with the candle in his hand, on the point of dying the death desired."

How else is she to describe her state now? She is a dying woman, with the candle of her faith in her hand; she is suspended upon the point of death. She cannot ask for a greater trial or a greater blessing than this. The agony she feels as she rises into the third stage is the agony of bliss too great to bear; she is wholly caught up in the presence of God, incapable of freeing herself from it even if she desired. There is no freedom to be found outside this ecstatic suffering, only the bondage of separation from His Majesty.

Words spill senseless from her tongue, beyond her power to order or understand. She babbles of her joy, begs God to cut her flesh and spirit into pieces, so that she may have the honour and the delight of enduring it for her Lord. Once, when she was a young girl, she desired to be martyred for her faith, and ran away from home to seek death at the hands of the Moors. She knew nothing then of martyrdom. Those who have died for the glory of Heaven have done but little; the strength by which they endured was the strength of their Father, and not their own. That strength overtakes her now, imprisons her, subjects her to sweetness that sears as hot iron.

And so passes the seventh day.

The pain vanishes in a blaze of light, one that sears her eyes like cool fire.

When her vision clears, a radiant figure stands before her. Its naked flesh is without mark, androgynous, in shape like a human and yet not. The light behind it is a suggestion of wings.

"Glory be to God in the highest," it says. The voice rings upon her ears, a carillon of bells, a blast of horns, deafening in its softness.

She prostrates herself upon the stone, not daring to look upon the angel.

"Rise," it says, both gentle entreaty and command. "You have refused the kindnesses we offered to you in previous guises, and so we come to you now in our true form. If you will not heed a friendly servant, a father, a priest, then heed *us*."

She lifts herself to her knees. The pain has returned, but in lesser form: the mere pain of dying, and not the sweet agony of God's presence. To be alone, even when in the presence of an angel, leaves her more desolate than any fleshly torment.

It is also a warning.

The words of the radiant figure roll like thunder through the room. "God does not desire your suffering. You bring it upon yourself, and call it a gift of the Lord. You spurn the true gifts He has given you: your intelligence you dismiss as foolishness, your strength of will you abandon as weakness. He gives you free will to choose virtue or sin, but you cast your virtues onto the dung-heap and declare yourself powerless to confront sin. Your humility is so great as to become arrogance."

That terrible voice stops, and silence falls. Then, more quietly, it asks, "What have you to say?"

She fixes her gaze upon the floor, refusing to gaze upon that light. "When I was in my youth," she says, "and began to experience visions of God, the priests around me were sore afraid. They believed my visions to be no true gift from Heaven, but a delusion sent by Satan, meant to lure me into damnation."

"They were no thing of Satan."

On that point they agree. She says, "I have feared this myself many times over the years, for I know I am a woman, and vulnerable to such fancies. But this reassurance I have: I know that Satan would not attempt to lure me into good behaviour, but would only encourage me toward sin. Therefore, if what my visions advised ran counter to what I knew of God's will, I would heed them not. I say *if*, for it did not occur. The visions were true."

Now, at last, she raises her eyes, confronting the creature before her directly. "Until now."

The wings shift and flare.

"You are no angel," she says, "but a false vision sent by the Devil. At this, the moment of my death, you hope to entrap me with soft words of kindness. His Majesty would not advise me so. And here is my proof: that He is not with me when you come."

A mere whisper from the creature is still enough to shake her bones. "I come to bring you God's mercy—which you have ever refused to accept."

She folds her hands in prayer, turns her attention to Heaven. And the light fades away, leaving a whisper of sorrow in its wake.

The cruelest torment she suffers is this: the awareness that she is not yet dead.

She does not wish to die so that her agony may end. If it went on for a hundred nights, she would praise the Lord. But so long as she lives, she is in the world, and is apart from His Majesty. How is such loneliness to be endured?

She cannot even think of it. God sweeps her up into the transformative union of prayer, the fourth and highest water; she is incapable of anything. Her tongue is silent, her body still. She cannot feel the stone beneath her shoulder where she has fallen, nor the fever that burns her from within, convulsing her limbs. Had she the ability to speak, to think, to will anything beyond that which His Majesty chooses to inflict, she would beg Him to pour this precious liquor into a more worthy vessel, shower his graces upon one who would do good with them instead of casting them into the mire. But the Lord, in His wisdom, chooses to show to her the depths of her worthlessness, by bringing her into the perfection of His self.

It could be an eternity. It comes near to being so. But as it always has before, the moment ends, and she is cast once more out into the world.

On the tenth day she is alone. Not even the false angel comes to visit her, in any guise.

She remembers her life, from its early, foolish days through her attempts to follow wisdom. How many hours and days did she squander in reading tales of knights! How much breath did she waste in conversation with friends, with kin, when she could have been speaking praise for the Lord! And how much joy came to her when she moved, however slowly, with however many stumbles, toward the truth: that to know God's love is to suffer.

Slowly, because of the weakness of her body, she stretches herself out upon the stone, lying prostrate. It may have been a lie of Satan that her suffering is to last for ten days, as the world outside moves to right its calculation of time. She does not know.

But either way, she will be prepared.

"Lord," she whispers to the stone, "either let me suffer, or let me die."

Words she has said many times before. Now, though, they are the purest expression of her faith.

And God answers her prayer.

She feels the agony of His presence coming upon her. With her last strength, she turns onto her back, facing Heaven.

The seraph descends, as it did once before, so many years before. In its hand it holds a golden spear with a fiery point, which it thrusts deep into her heart, penetrating her entrails. When the spear withdraws, all thought, all awareness vanish, burned to nothing in the blaze of perfect suffering.

When the morning came, they found her cold and quiet in her bed, the sheets about her soaked with sweat.

Her passing was an occasion of great mourning, for she had been a leader to many; and also of joy, for surely now she was with God. The word "saint" was on the lips of hundreds before the month was out. Not even thirty-two years passed before she was beatified; not even forty altogether before she was canonized. All the Catholic world knew of St. Teresa of Ávila, whose wisdom and holiness were a model to all.

But of this the saint knew nothing. She remains forever at the point of death: caught in the Hell she made for herself, and welcomed with tears of joy.

TO RISE NO MORE

PATRIXBOURNE, KENT: 1 April, 1828

"Come back here at once, you naughty child!"

The shouts faded into the spring air as Ada fled, laughing. When she gained the shelter of the trees, she slowed her pace; Miss Stamp would never follow her this far. She had tried once, the first time her charge vanished into the wood near the house at Bifrons, and had almost not found her way out again. To this day she swore the trees had moved when she wasn't looking, and Ada was not foolish enough to tell her the truth.

It was not nice to laugh at Miss Stamp, of course. She was in most respects an excellent governess. But it had become something of a game for Ada, creeping away when Miss Stamp was occupied to steal a precious few minutes out here.

She soon came to the edge of a little pond, well-shaded by the trees. Ada dug in the pocket of her shawl and removed a small bun, only slightly worse the wear for having resided there since breakfast. She placed it on a low stone at the edge of the pond and said to the air, "Oh no, an unattended piece of bread! What if something were to come and take it?"

"You have to do it *right*," a familiar voice complained from the trees. "Otherwise it won't work."

Ada turned a full circle, but saw nothing. "And what if I said you had to come out before I would do it right?"

The voice said tartly, "Then I would tell you that I have all eternity, and can wait. You, on the other hand, are mortal. You'll get hungry. And bored."

This was not far off the mark; by coming out here, Ada was missing lunch. "I could eat the bread myself."

"At which point there would be no reason for me to stay, would there?"

"Oh, very well." Ada picked up the bun, then laid it back down with an exaggerated flourish. "Out of the boundless generosity of my heart, I, the Honourable Augusta Ada Byron, do bestow upon the Good People of this wood—all one of her—this gift of mortal bread, to shelter her against iron, church bells, and other banes of this world."

She turned her back, as she had been instructed to do, and waited. The faintest scrape of noise came from behind her, and then, somewhat muddled by a full mouth: "You can look now."

The white dress of the girl standing by the rock was pristine, as if it had not travelled so much as six inches through the trees. Even its hem repelled the soil over which it trailed. When she arrayed herself on the stone, turning so the light coming through the branches struck her snowy hair, she looked as if she were sitting for a portrait. Only the bun in her hand and the bite she was chewing distracted from the image. The girl herself might have been only a little older than Ada's twelve years—if one did not look too closely at her eyes.

"Alarch," Ada said, "why do you never let me see you before you've eaten the bread?"

"Because it isn't comfortable," Alarch said. "Would you want someone to see you bare?"

Ada shrugged, unconcerned. "Miss Stamp does, when she helps me bathe."

"Yes, well, you are not my governess, and I am not bathing." Alarch bounced the bun in the palm of her hand. "But this is five bites, at least, so you will not have to turn your back again for some time. What shall we do today?"

Regretfully, Ada said, "I fear I cannot stay long. But I was hoping to measure your wings, so that I might see how large they are in proportion to your body."

Alarch rolled her eyes in amusement. "You know that I could

just charm you to fly, and you could skip all this tedious work."

"That would be cheating," Ada said, indignant. "I want to fly on my own, not because you made it happen. Besides, you wouldn't be able to charm me to fly in front of other people. Could you?"

Alarch looked thoughtful. Her eyes were the only dark thing about her, apart from her feet. Today those were pale, but sometimes she forgot and they remained a deep grey. "I might," she said, "so long as I had eaten tithed bread. But it's always tricky, when the charm goes on a human. Would you like me to try?"

"*No*," Ada said firmly. "Mama would hear of it, and I shudder to think what she would say. I expect she would blame it on my father, and then lock me up with mathematical books and never let me out again."

She did not mean it as a joke, but Alarch laughed anyway. "Your father! I wish I had met him. We aren't to blame for him, you know—at least, I don't think we are. Not every madman is the fault of the fae."

"Are you going to let me study your wings?" Ada asked. She really did not have much time to spare, but she also did not want to talk about her father. Lord Byron's death had not exorcised his ghost from her mother's mind, nor from her own. All it had done was remove the possibility that she might ever meet him—for her mother, fearing his madness, had left Lord Byron's household when Ada was only one month old.

It did not help to think that if she asked, one of Alarch's people might be able to call his ghost up for her to converse with.

"Very well," Alarch said, and put the bun down.

No matter how many times she watched it, Ada could not see how the transformation happened. Alarch stood up from the rock, but somehow when the motion ended, a swan was perched where the girl had been sitting.

The bird extended one wing. She was not, Ada thought, capable of sighing in that form, but if she could, she would have. Ada said, "You are a very good friend, to be so patient with me." She did not want the swan-maiden to think her ungrateful. "And your feathers are beautiful, though I know I have told you that before. I am hoping to make my own wings out of oil silk, which will be much easier to shape than feathers, but it will not be nearly so beautiful. Did I tell you, though, that I have thought of a way to fix them onto my shoulders?"

She continued chatting brightly while she took a knotted cord from her pocket and used it to measure first the swan's wing, then her body. The wing was easily a yard in length, and wiry with strength beneath the feathers; one buffet could have broken Ada's ribs. "I should take measurements from other birds as well, of course, as I think there must be variations between kinds. But I do not want to dissect anything. I will ask my mother for a book instead, one with plates to show me the anatomy. Or I have another idea, though I have not thought this one through very far, of fixing a steam engine to a sort of carriage, with enormous wings so that it can fly. But I think that would not be as enjoyable as flying on my own."

Ada did not need to mark her measurements down; she could hold them in her head easily enough. When she was done, Alarch shifted back into a girl. "A steam engine?" Alarch said, shuddering. "Ash and Thorn, what an unpleasant thought. All that iron."

"It isn't for faeries, goose," Ada said, using a branch to scrape the pond's bank clear of leaves and twigs. "It's for people. Mortals."

"Don't call me a goose."

Ada stopped. "I do beg your pardon. Miss Stamp has been calling me that a great deal lately. I have been calling myself a carrier pigeon ever since I began thinking about these wings, but Miss Stamp says I am only a silly goose."

This mollified Alarch, who watched as Ada began to sketch a wing into the cleared patch of dirt. "I will never understand that sort of thing," Alarch said after a time, gesturing at the sketch.

"It's only mathematics," Ada said, surveying her work. Her formal study of geometry was to begin soon, which would undoubtedly be of great use in this endeavour.

"Your mother a mathematician, all numbers and rationality;

your father a poet, all visions and madness. It's so romantic."
Alarch sighed, smiling.

Ada scowled at her. "It isn't romantic at all. They got along
dreadfully."

"No, but think of it! As if he were philosophic mercury and
she, philosophic sulphur. Opposites joined together to make
something greater than either one apart: the quintessence, the
philosopher's stone. Could that be you, do you think?" She gave
a conspiratorial wink.

"That's alchemy," Ada said, returning to her diagram, "and it
doesn't work."

"It doesn't work for *you*, perhaps."

It had not worked for her parents, either. They had been
opposites, but not the sort that could ever harmonize. And yet,
Ada refused to accept that such harmony was as impossible as her
mother believed. There must be a place for imagination, for
dreaming, even in mathematics. That conviction, as much as the
desire to soar through the air, was what inspired her to create
these wings—as proof of her concept, that the two ways of
thinking might work hand-in-hand. Numbers might build a way
to fly, but they would do nothing without the will to fly in the
first place, and that did not come from the rational part of her
mind.

No, it came from her association with a creature who was the
antithesis of rationality: a faerie swan-maiden, an immortal creature
who could be girl or bird at will, who could deceive a governess
with charms such that she could not even find her way out of a
small wood. Ill health had already sent Ada's mother to a doctor;
knowing that her daughter consorted with such impossibility
would shatter her entirely. It would be the final proof that
Byronic madness had won out over Milbanke sanity.

"You aren't mad," Alarch said quietly. She always denied
being able to hear people's thoughts, but she had an unsettling
knack for guessing Ada's.

Ada answered her with a half-smile and fiddled with a bit of
loose bark on her stick. "If I were, might I not imagine my faerie

companion reassuring me of my good sense?"

"Come to London," Alarch said. "I will introduce you to a hundred faeries and a dozen mortals who call them friend. Would that convince you that what you see is true?"

This at least persuaded Ada to laugh. "No, it would only convince me that London is full of madmen. Which I think is true in any event, whatever my own state may be. But I do not care if I am mad, so long as it allows me to fly."

"You will," Alarch said, with certainty. "And I will be there to see you soar."

Bifrons, Kent: 12 October, 1828

The ropes were gone from the house's "flying room," replaced by horse-tack and other oddments evicted from the stables by the arrival of their guests. Ada wandered among the clutter, fingers trailing across a piece of harness meant for a carriage. Might she not engage a harness-maker to craft the attachments for her wings? It would certainly be better than the ropes upon which she had swung thus far—especially now that those ropes had been removed.

She sighed. Unless she meant to pay the man in faerie gold, her mother would have to be the one to engage the harness-maker, and her health was still too poor for her to return to Bifrons. Once she saw how far Ada's plans had progressed, though...surely she would not chide her daughter for spending so much time and thought on the endeavour, when the proof of its feasibility lay before her.

"It is mathematics," Ada said stubbornly, addressing the piled equipment. "She should be pleased by that."

Her mother's sidesaddle lay atop a wooden frame in the room's far corner, just at the height of a pony's back. It took a few moments of experimentation for Ada to settle herself properly, but soon she was perched in the saddle. She bounced in place, imagining a pony trotting beneath her. It was not so good as she imagined flying would be, but it might be enjoyable to try.

When the door opened, it startled her. Ada's twitch caused the saddle to slip around the frame, and she fell heavily to the floor.

"My dear!" Miss Stamp rushed forward to help her up. "Are you hurt?"

"No, I am very well." In truth Ada's knee felt bruised, but she did not want Miss Stamp to worry.

She fussed over Ada regardless. "You did not hit your head, did you? No pain, no difficulty with your vision?"

Her questions made Ada go still. "No, Miss Stamp. I promise you, I am unhurt."

"That is a relief." Miss Stamp brushed her off, then turned to straighten the dangling saddle. "Were you pretending this was a horse? That is what it is called, you know—this sort of frame. But of course it is only a figure of speech."

Ada pressed her lips together. There was no doubt of it; something had put Miss Stamp on her guard. "Has my mother been writing to you? Does she think I am falling ill again?"

The pause in Miss Stamp's movements answered for her.

Falling ill *again*—as if she had been ill the first time. But at seven Ada had been too young to understand that she should hold her tongue about the things she saw. And perhaps some of it had been illness, too; the entire period was too muddled in her mind for her to say for certain. She only knew that it had begun with her seeing strange things out of the corner of her eye, and that speaking of it had sent her mother into a frenzy of concern. After that it was headaches and bed rest, a cessation of her studies, and then, just when Ada seemed to be recovering, that dream of her father. She presumed it was him, at least. A dark-haired man in a bed, whispering "Oh, my poor dear child! My dear Ada! My God, could I have seen her…give her my blessing…" Then, days later, word that Lord Byron had died in Greece.

She might have forgotten it all, dismissing it as nothing more than the fancies of an unwell mind, had her mother not taken this house at Bifrons. A house with a nearby wood, the wood with a pond, the pond with a resident swan-maiden. Proof that the things Ada had seen before were more than simple fancy.

"There is no reason for Mama to be concerned," Ada said. "I tell you, I am quite well."

Miss Stamp hesitated, then faced her. "Your behaviour has her worried. All this nonsense about making wings, the ropes strung up in this room, your supposed book of *Flyology*…"

No wonder Miss Stamp had come looking for her here. She and Ada's mother both thought this enterprise nothing more than a silly fancy, and "fancy" was a forbidden concept in this household. Why, Miss Stamp was even afraid of a simple metaphor—as if Ada would not be able to tell the difference between a wooden frame and an actual horse.

But saying so outright would only get her into trouble. If Ada was to win this battle, she would have to do so on her mother's terms. "It is mathematics," Ada insisted, as she had before. "Geometry. I am only thinking of how my lessons might be applied." And of what her lessons could achieve, when freed from the strictures her mother believed necessary—or inevitable.

"People cannot fly," Miss Stamp said firmly. "No equation can change that. You will only hurt yourself trying."

Faeries can fly, Ada thought, though she kept the rebellious thought to herself. *And I will find a way to do the same. I will show that Mama's world and my father's need not be wholly apart.*

Mortlake, Surrey: 17 February, 1829

"The swans here are very snobbish," Alarch said, sending a pebble skipping across the water of the Thames with a flick of her wrist. "They think that just because they are *royal* swans, that makes them superior to those of us from the countryside."

Ada sighed, watching the ripples dissipate in the chill grey water.

Alarch nudged her with one shoulder. "Why the long face? Are you worried for me? You needn't be. It would take more than some uppish swans to make me regret coming with you from Kent." She laughed at her own pun.

Unfortunately, it only made Ada more melancholy. The thought of Alarch being caught and marked during the annual swan upping was not to be borne—even though she knew her friend could easily escape by taking on human form.

Everything made her melancholy of late. Her mother's recurrent illness. The removal from Kent to Surrey. The loss of Miss Stamp, who had gone away to be married; the imposition of Miss Frend, who, though not engaged as Ada's governess, nonetheless over-saw her education with a strict and critical eye.

Her failure to fly.

Alarch regarded her with worried eyes. Ada made an effort to smile at her. "I am very glad to have you here."

"You have not asked to see my wings in ages," Alarch said. "I used to be annoyed that you would poke and prod at them…but now I find I miss it."

Ada shook her head, staring once more at the Thames. "I do not think what I had in mind will work. The size of the wing, if it is to be large enough to lift me—my body cannot possibly generate enough force to move it. Not with the speed required." Especially not when she kept growing. Every inch meant more weight for the wings to lift, without a commensurate gain in strength.

"What of your other notion? The steam-engine, with the carriage?"

Alarch must be concerned indeed if she, a faerie, was encouraging Ada to pursue such a prospect. Iron was poison to her very soul; the traditional tithe of bread only held that poison at bay, and then only for a while. Ada said, "It might work. But I do not have the mathematics necessary to design it."

Alarch laughed. "You will. Given the rate at which your mother is determined to teach you, it is only a matter of time."

A matter of time. Ada had already spent more than a year on this endeavour, and every passing day showed her how much further she was from her goal than she thought. When she was twelve, she had thought it would be done within the week. Now…even if she had a design that seemed effective, how was she to test it? A steam-engine could not be made in the parlour with wire and oil silk. And her mother would never fund the testing of such a thing, even if an engineer could be persuaded to try.

Alarch seized her hands. The faerie's grip was strong, a reminder of her powerful wings. However elegant her exterior, it hid something much tougher beneath.

"Listen to me," Alarch said, the intensity of her voice dragging Ada's attention from the river. "Do not let impossibility deter you. I have lived a thousand years and more, and seen mortals do things beyond the dreams of their ancestors. You build cities like great forests and people them with strange devices. You burn coal and boil water and somehow it drags unimaginable weight along a track. I do not understand how such an engine works, but I understand this: if humans can create such a thing, there is nothing they cannot do. It only wants the vision and tenacity to see it done. Your mother is nothing if not tenacious, but she would grind the vision from you if she could. *Do not let her.*"

The words made Ada's throat close up. *Vision* was not a thing she was supposed to have. That was a word for poets and madmen. But it burned within her regardless: the belief that her lessons were not—*should* not be—merely a discipline for her mind, a way to train her thinking to the bounds of rationality, but rather the means by which she might translate vision into reality. The wings on which her spirit would soar, even if her body could not.

Dizzy, she swayed where she sat.

Alarch's determination transformed to alarm. "Your hands— they are burning hot." She released one to lay her fingers against Ada's brow. "You are feverish. We should not have been out here in this cold wind. Come, we must get you home." She rose, drawing Ada with her.

Partway with her. The world spun, and Ada fell.

Mortlake, Surrey: 24 March, 1829

This time there were no dreams of her father.

There was only fever and sweating, itching and a cough that would not go away and would not let her sleep. She heard enough to understand that she had the measles, but everything past that was beyond her. Eating required too much effort. She swallowed broth only because her mother ordered her to, and obedience was a habit not easily broken. Besides, if she took the broth, then she would be left in peace, to fly on the wings of delirium.

In her fevered dreams she soared above the earth, seeing England wheel beneath her. There was no steam engine, no harness, not even any feathers. Human flesh and bone was enough. It had to be a charm, and she chided Alarch for placing it on her; had Ada not insisted she would fly on her own?

She saw the swan-maiden's face, white with worry. Always her friend had appeared in near-human guise, only small touches like the snowy sheen of her hair betraying her faerie nature, but what Ada saw now could never have been mistaken for mortal. The tolling of a nearby church bell made Alarch shudder, her hands clenching on Ada's shoulders.

"I cannot stay," Alarch said, the words echoing as if they came from a great distance away. "With no more bread—Ada, forgive me. I must return to Kent."

Kent. The fields and woods of Patrixbourne spun below her. She had tried so hard to fly above them, and now, at last, she succeeded.

"I will find you again," Alarch vowed. "Or you must come find me. Promise me, Ada. Do not let them make you forget us. Do not forget there is more to the world than your mother sees."

Someone began to hammer coffin nails. No, it was only footsteps in the corridor, and Ada was in her bed. Anguished, Alarch released her, and with a rustling of feathers she vanished.

✳

Here, then, our almost unfledg'd wings we try;
Clip not our pinions, ere the birds can fly:
Failing in this our first attempt to soar,
Drooping, alas! we fall to rise no more.

—"An Occasional Prologue"
Lord Byron

✳

Chelsea, London: 5 June, 1833

The Somervilles' house was not nearly so elegant as others Ada had visited of late, being a dreary government residence, provided to them as part of Dr. Somerville's appointment to Chelsea Hospital. Laid against the glittering beauty of Court, at which Ada had been presented not a month past, it seemed a positive dungeon.

Appearances were misleading. Ada would not have traded this cramped little place for Clarence House itself. The company here was far more congenial.

Mary Somerville greeted her with a broad smile and a brief embrace. "I am so glad you could join us," she said, tucking her hand inside Ada's arm. "You are looking splendidly well."

"I feel as if I have my strength back at last," Ada said. "I hardly recognized myself when I climbed from my sickbed—and indeed, I hardly recognize myself now, for I am not the same person I was when I fell ill." More than two years on bed rest would change anyone, but those years had also carried her over the threshold into womanhood.

No, nothing so definite as womanhood. She had felt like a soft mass of dough, that needed shaping into *some* kind of form. Riding had strengthened her wind and shed some of the weight brought on by enforced idleness, while preparations for her presentation at Court last month had polished an exterior long since grown dull. Mr. Turner...

Best not to think of that indiscretion. Her tutor was gone; she must accept the loss. Pursuing him had been the height of irrationality to begin with, and she should have known better.

"You are recovered now," Mary said, squeezing her arm, "and your mother tells me your studies go very well."

"They resume, at least, which is a positive victory after these last few years. I found it dreadfully hard to concentrate," Ada admitted. "The smallest things would overwhelm me. But I have begun to refresh my memory on geometry and algebra, and as soon as my grip on those is secure once more, I will continue onward."

By now the maid had taken Ada's bonnet and mantle, and so Mary drew her toward the parlour. "I know you had an interest in astronomy, before you fell ill. Is that still the case?"

She might as well have asked what transpired before the Flood. Thinking back that far was like reaching through a fog, like trying to grasp smoke. "It is a good use for mathematics," Ada said vaguely as they entered the parlour. "Mama told me you translated Laplace's *Mécanique Céleste* while I was ill. I have not yet had the time to read it."

Mary clicked her tongue. "No, of course not, poor child. But one of our guests tonight helped Mr. Herschel found the Astronomical Society, and won its Gold Medal—oh, eight years ago, now? No, nine. Come, let me introduce you."

She led Ada across the room to where three men stood in conversation. Or rather, one was expounding at length, and the other two were listening. "All you need is addition and subtraction," he insisted. "Simple processes, not complex ones. Finite differences, don't you see? Say you have a polynomial function—"

One of the gentlemen looked as if he wished to interject a question but was too polite to interrupt. Mary Somerville was not so hesitant. "Mr. Babbage," she said, "I will stop you there, so that this young lady may listen in without eavesdropping. May I present to you the Honourable Miss Ada Byron? Ada, these gentlemen are Mr. Henry Chapman, Mr. William Raine, and Mr. Charles Babbage."

The gentlemen bowed, and Mr. Babbage kissed her hand with a distracted air. "Eavesdropping? Are you another mathematical sort, then, like Mrs. Somerville here?"

Ordinarily when people heard Ada's name, their minds went directly to her notorious father. She was at once pleased and obscurely disappointed that the connection did not seem to occur to Mr. Babbage. "I am a mere student of mathematics," she said. "But what little knowledge I have is great enough to make me curious. What is it you were saying about finite differences?"

He cocked an eyebrow at her, as if surprised by her interest. "I was explaining the operation of my Difference Engine, which can calculate mathematical tables by that method."

"For astronomy?" Ada asked, thinking of Mary's words.

Babbage gestured expansively, nearly striking the man to his right. "For any purpose in which mathematics might be of use. And what cannot be helped along with numbers?"

It called up a nameless ache, which Ada concealed as Mary presented her to the other two gentlemen. She did not want to worry anyone. There was no reason to fear a relapse of her illness; she was fully recovered. No more fevers, no more visions of things that were not there. Her mad passion for her tutor had been a child's foolishness, now put aside, along with the fancies of her childhood. She was her mother's daughter, not her father's.

But for some reason, that thought made the ache worse.

Babbage was only too happy to answer her questions about the Difference Engine; indeed, his delight grew with each one she asked. When pressed, he admitted it might have utility for astronomy, military endeavours, even music. All the world, reduced to numbers.

No, not reduced, Ada thought—it struck her so forcefully, she almost said it out loud. *Revealed.*

His words threw open a window in her mind, admitting a gust of wind that blew away the stale and stuffy air of her long illness. She hesitated upon the threshold of a neglected room, unsure whether to enter or back away, feeling as if to go in would bring her back to that dreadful time—to delirium and madness, losing touch with the world she had struggled so hard to regain.

But every word coming from Mr. Babbage's mouth seemed to jostle her, threatening to tip her over that threshold. He might love numbers for their own sake, but Ada found herself thinking that mathematics was a means to an end, not an end in and of itself. Her mother used the subject to bridle Ada's rebellious mind...but did not a bridle allow one to ride a horse? And then the rider could travel anywhere she wished to go.

Against her better judgment, Ada found herself saying, "I once thought to use numbers to find a way to fly."

"And why not?" Babbage said, unperturbed by the interruption.

"Well, I can think of several reasons why not. It didn't turn out very well for Icarus, if the Greeks are to be believed. But that's the general idea, yes. The Difference Engine is only a start—though one I'm rather proud of. I already have several ideas for improvements. More complex engines, for more complex purposes. If someone comes up with the equation for flight, my machines will be able to calculate the answer."

She laughed, cheeks heating with embarrassment. "It was a girlhood dream, Mr. Babbage, and I am now a woman grown. But I should very much like to see this Engine. Perhaps if I continue my studies, I could provide some little assistance to your efforts."

The offer was presumptuous in the extreme, but Babbage's wide smile told her he did not mind. "It's rare enough for me to find anyone who understands the mathematics of the thing in the first place, Miss Byron, let alone dreams of uses for them. I have the Engine in a shed out behind my house; you're welcome to come view it."

Ada found herself short of breath, as she had not been for many months. A distracted part of her mind said that she should excuse herself and sit down, but she did not move. This entire conversation, pairing dreams and equations, echoed in her memory like a long-forgotten tune. *Philosophic mercury and philosophic sulfur,* Ada thought, and wondered why she had thought of alchemy.

For an instant, her vision swam. She had an impression that the spritely gentleman Mary had introduced as Mr. Raine looked very different: thin as a stick and quite tall, with eyes too blue for any human man. A silly fancy, and one that would appal her mother.

Mr. Raine gave her a peculiar smile and said, "Mr. Babbage is prone to driving off the layman with his abstruse 'explanations.' But with someone like you, Miss Byron, to help translate him to the world…I imagine you could do great things together."

With a feeling of shaking the dust of past ages from her skirts, Ada dismissed his strange appearance. Not the sight of it—that remained—but the concern it ought to engender. What did it matter, truly? Ada was seventeen years of age, and could tell the difference between fancy and reality. Moreover, she could judge for herself how best to mix the two.

After all, a little bit of irrationality was necessary to fly.

She smiled at Mr. Babbage. "Let us see if Mr. Raine is correct. I am eager to discover what what this Engine of yours is capable of."

FALSE COLOURS

THE SKIES WERE CLEAR and the winds fair for Plymouth, the *Hesperides* flying before them like a swan, her wings unfurled from the yardarms and belling out full. On deck, the gusts were strong enough to flick sailors' tarred tails of hair forward over their shoulders; higher in the rigging, they were strong enough to knock my shoulders forward and test the set of my feet on the rope beneath. I grinned into the afternoon sky, momentarily letting the wind carry my concerns from me, away into the distance, as if to drown them in the deep.

I loved these moments aloft. The mast swayed in great arcs with the pitch and roll of the ship below, which had alarmed me greatly in my midshipman days. Now I found it exhilarating. And it was one of the few places aboard a frigate where one could feel truly alone.

Nearly three hundred men on the *Hesperides*, packed in cheek by jowl, and a trifle bloodied by our work at Algeciras two weeks before. But good spirits prevailed: our squadron had sunk two Spanish vessels and captured a French seventy-four, with scarcely more than a dozen killed on our side. It was remarkable how rapidly a decent victory could improve morale.

A decent victory, and the prospect of shore leave ahead. Our harbour was approaching, visible on the horizon without need for the spyglass thrust into my breeches. Duty called, as it always did. I called down to the deck in a strong bellow, then gripped the backstay in my calloused hands, piked my body upward to wrap my legs over, and slid down the thick rope with practised ease.

Perkins was waiting for me below, hat in hand. I accepted my cover from the midshipman with a nod and, settling it upon my head, made my way aft through the routine bustle of sailors and ropes, all the bones and sinews and blood that kept the ship in flight across the waves. The *Hesperides* was more battered than her men; a thirty-two gun frigate had no business in a battle between ships of the line. But broken yardarms, splintered deck planks, shattered rails—those could all be repaired, and would be. Leave would give us time to rest, and everyone was eager to get to it.

Except the lieutenants of the *Hesperides*, who faced a different fate. I found Harry brooding on what remained of the taffrail, broad shoulders hunched inside his coat, sea-coloured eyes slitted against the force of the wind. "Plymouth in sight," I said, as if he might not have noticed, and got only a grunt in response. "It's only a party, Harry."

It gained me a half-smile. "I thought you hated parties."

I did. They were invariably attended by mothers with unmarried daughters, who saw a promising young lieutenant as a reasonably likely prospect. Dedicated rakes might enjoy that game, but as Britain's least eligible bachelor, I found it nothing short of torture. Still—"It's good to get off the ship once in a while."

"Never long enough to see your sister, though. Does it bother you?"

"I wish Victoria's health were good enough to allow her to come south," I said. "But the mail packet should bring another letter, which is always good." It meant my arrangements were still holding.

"No Almack's for her," Harry said, his gaze still fixed outward. "No society at all, for an invalid. It must be hard."

I found it odd that he should say so. Neither of us had ever been to Almack's—though one heard the tales, even out at sea. Did he miss the elegance of that life?

For my own part, I did not. This was what I loved best: sails and rigging, rudder and hull, the salt spray peeling at my face. Life on land would be safer, for sure—I never yet heard of a dancer at Almack's losing a hand or leg to someone's misstep—but with less of glory in it, and less *purpose*.

I did not voice these thoughts to Harry. There was no need: he and I were joined in our love for the sea and the service that commanded our loyalty. He was my dearest companion in all the world, and I, if I did not miss my guess, was his. We had been friends since my first day as a midshipman, and had hardly been separated since, excepting my brief and ill-fated assignment to the *Persephone*. We understood each other even without words.

Usually. Yet I had no idea what troubled him today.

From behind us came a familiar, hated voice. "Looking ahead to the whores? There will be none for us. Fine ladies instead, much good may it do."

If I had little need to share my thoughts with Harry, I had even less desire to do so with Byrom. But I did not like having him at my back, and so turned to face *Hesperides'* second lieutenant. "You'd prefer Plymouth's pox-ridden women? Myself, I'd sooner lick the sores of a leper—it would be safer for my health."

A faint, supercilious smile often lurked about Byrom's mouth. Now it grew nastier. "Indeed. Perhaps your preferences lie elsewhere, Ravenswood."

My back went rigid. For words like that, I could call him out, and any man alive would call it justice. But if I did....

Byrom knew his hold over me, and missed no opportunity to exert it.

Rage boiled in my veins, less for the present insult—merely the newest in a long series—and more for the despicable position into which I had fallen. The thought had even entered my head, during the battle, whether it might not be worth the cost to shoot Byrom where he stood. Him, and then myself: I almost believed I had rather endure hell's punishment for a suicide than the ordeal I suffered now. Though if the devil had any sense of irony, my punishment would be exactly what I sought to escape.

I received the bosuns' yells with gratitude, for they broke me from my black and murderous thoughts, summoning me to my work. Without speaking, I pushed past Byrom and went to do my duty.

Harry followed me down to the ship's waist. In a voice I hoped was not clear to the men's ears, he said, "Honestly, Simon—no one could fault you if you called him out."

"Granger doesn't like his officers to duel," I said, pausing to let some of the men swing up onto the ratlines, heading aloft to reef sail.

"But he's given you no command against it."

"That's a lawyer's argument, Harry, and unlike you."

He winced, and I regretted the barb. But the anger in his tone wasn't directed at me. "*I* should like to see you call him out."

If only I could. But Byrom would never accept the challenge. "The Navy's golden boy? Lowry wouldn't like it if I damaged his future lieutenant." Much less killed him, as he deserved. The rage flared up again.

"They intend him for promotion, obviously," Harry agreed. "Lowry takes prizes aplenty, and gives their command to his officers; the Admiralty rarely revokes the promotions. They say the *Inimitable* may be the finest ship our yards have turned out. Lowry will be in a hurry to test that."

Which meant Byrom might be a commander within a year, and a post-captain soon after. I wondered if God had placed me in this position as punishment for my sin. But why wait so long to inflict it? And why punish innocents along with me?

Determined to turn my thoughts from their course, I bent to the task of bringing the ship into port. "Never mind Byrom. Let's go to meet our doom."

Our doom consisted of genteel music, finely-dressed gentlemen and ladies…and one face whose unexpected presence struck me with the force of a musket ball.

Lady Katherine Deverell stood beside her husband in elegant lace, her hair coiffed in the latest fashion, greeting her guests with a smile and the graceful extension of one gloved hand. All that gentility was as good as a disguise, compared with the hoyden she had been, years before; and yet I should have recognised Kate Lyon were she painted like a harlequin.

Her eyes fixed on me even before Captain Granger finished his introductions. There was no way she could fail to remember the name of Simon Ravenswood; it had not been so many years as that. But how much did she guess?

"You seem to know the gentleman," Lord Deverell said, noticing Kate's interest—as any man might who has fifteen years on his pretty young wife and knows it.

I spoke before she could. "The lady and I were acquainted in childhood," I said, my tone cordial but distant, to lay her husband's fears to rest. "Before she went to Italy. She was good friends for a time with my sister Victoria. We have not seen each other in many years."

Kate's eyes narrowed. But she could hardly say anything, not there in front of everyone, and I felt mixed relief and regret as we made polite small talk and then moved away so that she and her husband could greet their other guests. Either, I supposed, would be short-lived; I could hardly avoid her for the entire night. Whether I wanted to or not...that question, I could not answer.

Nor did I have time to consider it. Before long, I had another matter to distract me.

I had met Harry's family before, and greeted Mrs. Wycliffe and her daughter with a smile and a well-practised bow over their hands. The third lady with them, however, was unknown to me. "Lt. Ravenswood, may I present Miss Charlotte Fanning?" Mrs. Wycliffe said, ushering the girl forward. She beamed fondly at Miss Fanning. "Harry's fiancée."

Despite my self-control, I stuttered visibly in my bow. Fortunately, the angle concealed my expression from the ladies; I could only hope Harry himself had not been watching. By the time I straightened, my look was one of pleased surprise. "Harry said nothing to me of an engagement!"

It was not the best response. Miss Fanning smiled awkwardly; no young lady would like to hear that her husband-to-be has kept her a secret. But Mrs. Wycliffe gave her son an indulgent pat on the arm. "He is dreadfully superstitious. I cannot deny that the life of a naval lieutenant is a dangerous one, and difficult for his family. I'm sure your own sister feels the absence keenly, Lt. Ravenswood. But it's nonsense to think that speaking of good news will bring ill fortune in return."

Superstitious? No more than any sailor. Why had Harry not said anything of this to me? We might leave a great many things unspoken, knowing the other would fill in what had not been said, but this was close-mouthed even for him. I was not some dockside fortune-teller, to ferret out secrets I had not been told.

He would not meet my gaze, either, when I glanced at him. Well, he could hardly offer an explanation here, in front of the others. But I would have to press him for one later.

I realised by the faltering smiles of the ladies that I had let myself fall into too long of a silence. To Miss Fanning, I said, "My felicitations to you both. If Harry is half so attentive to his duties in marriage as he is in the Navy, you will be well situated indeed."

Even as I said the words, I winced inwardly; that was not the most graceful compliment I had ever offered. It seemed I was doomed to spend my evening shifting from one awkwardness to another.

I should have trusted that thought. It would not have saved me, but it would at least have prevented me from feeling such misplaced relief when Granger drew me away. "There is someone you should meet," the captain said, leading me across the room. His next words put a leaden weight in my stomach. "You and Byrom both."

He collected the second lieutenant and guided us to another group of women, four in number. One older, and three younger: they looked familiar, though I had not met them before. As soon as Granger introduced them, I understood why. It took no dissembling at all to show the pain I felt as I said, "Ma'am, my sincere condolences on the loss of your son."

Mrs. Warrington gave my hand the tiniest squeeze as I released hers. "I'm glad to make your acquaintance at last, Lt. Ravenswood. Percy wrote often of you in his letters. He considered you his greatest friend aboard the *Persephone*."

He had his eyes from his mother, I saw, a warm and trusting

brown. All his sisters shared them, too. To face his family en masse, with Byrom standing rigid at my side...I wondered what Percy Warrington had written of *him*.

Byrom was too canny to show that side of himself so publicly, though. With smooth courtesy, he said, "It was an honour to serve with your son, Mrs. Warrington. One of many fine men lost that day."

His platitude made me grit my teeth. These ladies deserved better than such empty words. "I don't know if you were aware, ma'am," I said, "but Captain Monmouth intended that he should stand for lieutenant at the next opportunity. I have no doubt he would have passed."

The possibility of tears glimmered at the corners of her eyes, but she held her sorrow in. "Thank you, Lt. Ravenswood; it is very kind of you to say so. We desired nothing more than that he should serve with valour."

Nothing more than that he should serve, and return home safely. I tried to block out the memory of his face, and failed.

The eldest Miss Warrington twisted her fan in her fingers and said hesitantly, "If—if I may—"

You may not, I wanted to say, for I could read in her expression the words that were coming. And would have rather faced a French broadside, armed with nothing but a knife.

"Could we beg you to tell us what happened? To the *Persephone*, I mean."

My gut clenched. "The account of it was published in the *Gazette*."

An account I knew by heart, for it was a digest of my own words to the Admiralty. I kept a copy next to my heart, the paper much battered with folding, and even now it seemed to burn a hole through my ribs. The mother laid one hand on her daughter's arm—not to quell her, but to take up her cause. "The *Gazette* says so little, though, only the barest outline—"

"That is a kindness to the families," I said, my fingers curling tight. "The details are not something ladies should hear."

"Please, lieutenant," she said with quiet dignity. "He was my only son. No insult intended to Lt. Byrom, whose conduct was so gallant—but you were such a friend to Percy; I had rather hear it from you."

I had no need of suicide to place me in hell. I was there already. But worse than this would be to allow the unsuspecting Mrs. Warrington to hear the tale from *him*.

Byrom stood at my side, a grenade ready to go off if I made the slightest error.

Fixing my gaze in the distance, and hoping they would credit the tension in my voice to the unpleasantness of the memory, I opened my mouth and lied.

I fled as soon as I could afterward, out of that elegant hall where I did not belong in the slightest. How I found my way to the gardens, I could not say, for no one had shown me the path, but the next thing I was aware of was the fresh evening air. It cleared my head, though my stomach still roiled with sick shame and fury.

Oh God, the lies stuck in my throat, clawing it bloody. I had thought myself at my deepest nadir when I stood before an Admiralty board and gave my word of honour that the demise of the *Persephone* had gone as I said, leaving myself and the heroic Lt. Byrom as its only survivors. But that was nothing, *nothing* compared to this: lying to the face of a grieving mother.

Cold comfort that Percy had behaved with every bit of valiance and honour I imputed. Far more than *I* showed now. And yet, what other choice did I have?

None. Byrom had me trapped, as effectively as if he held a pistol to my head. He could make me crawl, make me relinquish the name of gentleman—everything I had built up for myself, he could and did strip away from me, leaving me a despicable, dishonourable *thing*.

"*Victoria!*"

The name, hissed just over the rush of the breeze, snapped me back to alertness like a gunshot. Someone else had come into the gardens.

I had not survived so long in the Navy, however, without developing strong nerves. I startled, but no more than anyone might upon being surprised, and turned where I stood on the path, boots crunching in the gravel. As if I did not know who I would see.

Kate hurried to join me, tugging her pelisse up to cover her bare arms. "Don't worry," she said as she drew near. "No one else is out here. I am not such a fool as to say anything where another might hear. Oh, Victoria, it *is* you!"

My heart skipped a beat every time she said the name—a name I had scarcely heard in ages, scarcely even dared *think*, lest thought lead to action, and action betray. If Byrom's gaze threatened my carefully constructed facade, Kate's voice stripped it away, revealing the truth that lay behind: not Simon Ravenswood, but Victoria.

Kate's eyes danced in merriment as she halted before me. "I couldn't believe it when I saw you, that you would have the cheek to show up in such a fashion—oh, you must tell me what is going on! Where is Simon?"

There was no possibility of lying. Kate would never believe me if I pretended she was mistaken, and would be insulted if I tried. My mouth was as dry as bone. I heard my own voice as if it were a stranger's: habitually at the lower edge of my range, low enough to pass for a man's light tenor. "Dead."

The merriment in her eyes staggered, faded, died. "What? But why haven't you—" Understanding dawned, as she remembered why my twin had entered the Navy to begin with. "The inheritance."

I nodded.

"But Victoria, to pretend to be Simon—I know we played at it when we were young, masquerading as boys, but he's a lieutenant; they will catch you out—" Again the flow of words stuttered to a halt. Her lips parted in amazement, or perhaps horror, as she realised her own error. "How—how long have you been doing this?"

The number startled even me, when I spoke it. "Six years. He died during his first leave."

I saw her look at me again, this time seeing not Victoria, but Lt. Ravenswood. My weathered skin, my sinewy hands, my hair in its rough tail, the dark strands glinting reddish-brown where the sun and wind had bleached them. The heavy wool of the coat hid the rest: the scars of battle, the whipcord strength where feminine softness should have been. I made a spare man, but so would my twin have done. Taking after our father as we did, I had little that needed concealing.

"Heavens, Victoria," Kate whispered, staring frankly. "How have you *done* it?"

Wryness twisted my mouth into an unfamiliar smile. "With difficulty."

She covered a giggle with her hand, and waved for me to go on.

The wind tugged strands of hair into my face. "It's possible to get privacy on board a ship, though far from easy. And you can even piss standing up, if you know the trick—" I broke off, wincing. "I'm sorry."

"Not at all," Kate managed, despite her ladylike blanch. "Though now I *do* believe you've been six years in the Navy."

I looked away in embarrassment. No need to tell her the other graphic details. I was fortunate that my nature, or perhaps the physical strain of my life, made my blood come rarely. "Officers rarely strip down, not like the men. And I have done my d—my best to avoid any error that might lead to corporal punishment. They would know me quickly enough, if I removed my shirt."

"But to attempt such a masquerade in the first place…." She wrapped her pelisse more tightly.

"I panicked," I admitted, barely loud enough to hear. "Without Simon, I had nothing. No future, nor any hope of one. Our uncle's terms were quite clear: we received our stipends only so long as Simon was in the Navy, and the rest of the money would come only when he made post. Absurd, to think I could take his place—and yet it was the only thing I could think of."

Kate sank down onto a bench, still dazed. "Hannah Snell did it; why not you? Though she was a Marine, which I suppose is different. And a woman grown, not a twelve-year-old child." She shuddered, likely at the thought of my youth. "However did you manage?"

"What choice did I have? When I came back I told them I had fallen from my horse and struck my head; it can damage the memory. I had bought those books before Simon went away, to learn what he would be doing—"

"Sailing manuals," Kate said, nodding. "I remember."

Manuals I had studied obsessively—far more obsessively than my twin did. "I knew names from his letters, and put them to faces when I reported back. It was enough—though hard going at first."

"And so you've been trapped all this time," she murmured, touching my wrist in sympathy.

"Trapped?" The word felt odd on my tongue. "I suppose that in the early days, I saw it that way. I made a rash decision, and had no way out of it; I could not desert, they would not release me from the service, and to admit the truth would be worse than continuing to lie. Had it not been for Harry—Lt. Wycliffe—I don't know if I could have endured it."

Her gaze sharpened at the name. "Does he know?"

I shook my head, perhaps a touch too vehemently. "He is my dearest friend, but no. I could never tell him."

Kate raised one eyebrow, as if she heard something in my tone. I was not about to admit, even to her, the incident that occurred—or rather, *nearly* occurred—the night I was made lieutenant. Harry and I had both been drunk, which was both cause and cover; I did not think he remembered how close we came to kissing.

She allowed the issue to rest, but her next question was nearly as awkward. "What will you do when you are made post? Will you stay? I imagine it would be easier for a captain to keep secrets."

It would. But I could not tell Kate the true answer: that I had no hope of success. Even if I escaped disgrace, there were hordes of lieutenants in the Navy, all competing for a far smaller number of commands. I lacked the political connections that could aid me, and without them, I might never get my step.

Movement caught my attention. We were no longer alone in the gardens; several figures had come out onto the terrace. What excuses Kate had made to follow me I did not know, but we could not go on like this, talking so privately. Her husband would begin to wonder, if he did not already. Feeling both relieved and reluctant, I said, "We should go."

Kate caught my sleeve as I stepped away. "Victoria—"

My face hardened. "You must not call me that."

"Simon, then—Lt. Ravenswood." Her lips quirked on the name, but only in passing. "Quickly—does *anyone* here know?"

I offered my arm again, and she took it smoothly, as if I were any gentleman. How much should I admit to? "Granger," I said under my breath.

"Your *captain?*"

"I was wounded—a shot to the thigh." All of this sotto voce, as we crossed toward the house. "I didn't witness the scene myself, being unconscious, but at that range the ship's surgeon could hardly miss the truth. He told Granger."

Kate pinked again. She didn't use to be this easily embarrassed; all that schooling in Italy had wrought changes. "What did he do?"

"Told the surgeon to dig the bloody thing out before I took an infection, and he would address the matter when I woke. By the time I did, Granger had decided to let me stay."

An oversimplification, but we were too close to the other guests for me to relate the rest of it. In actuality, Granger had listened to my story, while I quaked in my skin. Then he told me, in deceptively level tones, that I would be testing for lieutenant at the next opportunity. After I failed, he would have me out of the service on terms that would save him the awkwardness of explaining how a young woman had got past him all that time.

But I had not failed. And I wondered sometimes whether Granger had ever expected me to.

"You tell the tale so prettily," Byrom murmured in my ear a while later, knowing it would stick under my skin like a barb. I turned my back on him and walked away, but it did no good; I could feel the pressure of his satisfaction on me like a weight. With the Warringtons giving me tearful smiles whenever I passed, by the time Harry drew me aside, I was more than ready to play the bear.

"I'm sorry," he said, pacing the side parlour to which we had retired. "I should have told you long since. About Miss Fanning."

My answer came sharp. "No, I quite understand. It is a private matter, not to be shared with outsiders."

"Damn it, Simon!" He rounded on me, hands clenching. "That isn't it, and you know it. I cannot think of anyone less an outsider to me than you. We were snivelling middies together; you've been covered in my blood, and I in yours. We might as well be brothers."

Harry's words put a cramp in my gut. Talking with Kate had been a mistake; it made me Victoria in my own mind, twitching every time Harry called me Simon. And for him to call me *brother....*

What I wanted was impossible, and I knew it. Even before the arrival of the unfortunate Miss Fanning. But that did not stop me from wanting it.

The tightness in my throat made my voice come out dangerously high. "Then why not tell me? Our friendship—" I forced myself to say it. "Our *brotherhood* has rarely been a thing of words. We understand one another without them. But an engagement is a devil of a thing to leave unspoken."

Harry's shoulders sagged inside the heavy wool of his coat. "I...oh, hell. Mrs. Fanning is a dear friend of my mother's. They both wanted the match, and I thought...I don't know what I thought."

I damned the lightness that rose inside my chest. "Don't you wish to marry her?"

"It hardly matters, now," Harry said unhappily. "I've asked

for her hand; I can hardly take that back."

No, he could not. No more than I could take back the rash decision that had put me on board the *Hesperides*. Even though it meant Harry knew Victoria Ravenswood only as a fiction, a sickly sister living in rural penury. But would he have given her a second thought, had she never donned the mask I wore now?

We made our decisions, and then we lived with them. Both of us were too honourable to do otherwise. "I'm sure it will be all right. You're a good man, Harry, and I'm sure she's a good woman. There are worse foundations for a marriage."

"And better ones, too," he said, gazing downward in dejection. But it did not last: he straightened his shoulders, donning once more the martial bearing we had both learned to maintain, and we went back out to the party.

Where I caught Byrom's gaze, narrowed in suspicion that I had withdrawn with Harry. A hint of a leer bent his thin mouth, and had I been in range at that moment, I would have smashed it with my fist.

My fury, thwarted of its target, bent back upon myself. Had I not just been congratulating myself on how honourable Harry and I were? For him, it might be true, but never for myself. My eyes were drawn, as if by a magnet, to the Warrington sisters and their mother. I had lied to their faces. I had no honour left. I had allowed Byrom to strip it from me, out of cowardice and shame.

There is a kind of madness that takes a man—or a woman—when the call comes to leap from the deck of one ship to another, boarding for the chance of a prize. With Marines shooting from the tops and the cutlasses of the enemy waiting, a man must be mad to fling himself across that gap. And yet time and time again he does it, out of optimism or patriotism, for bloodlust or for a cause, but most often of all for one simple reason: he cannot bear the thought of seeming a coward before his friends and comrades. His honour requires him to charge into the teeth of his own destruction.

Sometimes he may hope to emerge unscathed. I had no such expectation. But with Harry promised to Miss Fanning, and Byrom about to be rewarded for his crimes, I found I could no longer bear the weight of my own dishonour. With the madness of battle boiling in my veins, I went in search of Captain Granger.

We two, at least, could speak in private without occasioning comment. We returned to the garden, not far from where I had walked with Kate; I found it easier to breathe in the free air.

This might be one of my last chances to enjoy it.

"I apologise for troubling you, sir," I said, locking my hands behind my back to keep them from trembling. "A party is neither the time nor place for a matter of this sort, but I fear I cannot, for my own conscience, keep silent any longer."

Granger grew still, as I had seen him do a thousand times before: a flicker sighted in fog, an unidentified mast on the horizon, that might yet prove dangerous. The last time he had directed such alert study toward me, I was a midshipman, unable yet to stand for the wound in my thigh, explaining to him why I had chosen to masquerade as my twin brother.

When a thing must be done, it is better to do it quickly. I had learned *that* lesson from our ship's surgeon. "The account I have given of Byrom's actions aboard the *Persephone* is false."

The rest of the words poured out of me as if I had rehearsed them: crisp and dispassionate, a lieutenant's report on an unsuccessful naval engagement. But this time, instead of the positioning of the ships and the set of the wind with respect to the nearby shore, I spoke of the incompetence and cowardice of the *Persephone*'s first lieutenant, the despicable Edmund Byrom. I could not lay the loss of the ship and her men entirely at his feet; we'd had a damnable run of bad luck, before and during the battle with the *Aigrette*. But from his actions as officer of the watch to his final, despicable flight, Byrom had disgraced himself and the service. And I would rather cut my own throat than allow him to hold command over men once more.

Granger kept silent through my recitation, not even asking for clarification on any point. When I finished, he stood facing the wind, jaw set in a hard line. I knew what he would say, and braced myself for it.

"You lied to the Admiralty. Why?"

My own failings were harder to voice. But I had begun; I must continue. "When we washed up on the Spanish shore…I lost consciousness. Byrom went through my clothing, looking for anything of value or use, and discovered my secret. When I woke, he presented his demands: I must help him to safety, and afterward must never speak a word of his errors. I must present him as a hero—say that he fought valiantly to save the *Persephone*, and was responsible for saving me. If I did not, he would expose me as a woman."

"And what makes you tell the truth now?"

I bent my head, unable to stand straight while I admitted it. "The Warrington family. Lying to them…I must write a letter, I think. With the true story. Nothing of what I said regarding Percy was false, but they deserve to know who should be blamed for his death."

"You think you will have the opportunity to write a letter." This voice, too, I had known before; Granger used it when his fury must be private, rather than bellowed to the world. The surgeon had cleared the infirmary and its surroundings before the captain came to see me, but I do not think anyone would have heard his words if they were standing on the other side of the curtain. They were intended for one set of ears only, and fell upon them like hammers. "I protected you, Ravenswood. And this is how you repay me."

My eyes closed, of their own accord; I forced them open again. "I am sorry, sir. Which means very little, and I know it. But the only compensation I can make is to ensure that Byrom is disgraced as he deserves, whatever the cost to myself."

He grunted. "Whatever the cost. I told you before that you could be hanged for what you have done; you would be dependent upon the leniency of the court, and their wish not to be seen as laughing-stocks, for any lesser punishment. But now you have lied to an Admiralty board. They will execute you for that."

"Sir...." How could I put it into words? I could not. Some parts of it Granger should not hear anyway. He would not want to know the role Miss Fanning had played in sending me to this desperate end. But some parts I could say. "If I did not speak, Byrom would have more chances to get men killed. Should I value my life above theirs?"

Granger exhaled sharply, not quite a snort. "A very noble sentiment. Do you actually mean it?"

My back went rigid. "Sir. Ever since I took my brother's place, I have striven at all times to serve His Majesty's Navy as the best officer I can be. The immutable fact of my sex has always undermined that; I am a woman, and I must lie about that fact, and both those things make me less than a gentleman. But I have done my utmost to behave as a gentleman in every other respect, to counterbalance those flaws by the perfect execution of my duties. Byrom took that from me: he provoked me into weakness and cowardly self-preservation. If making restitution for that failure costs me my life, then I will pay it gladly."

Granger met my gaze for a long, wordless time; then he let his breath out in a sigh and shook his head. "Damn it, Ravenswood. You're a better gentleman than most whose sex and birth gives them that name. When I sent you to test for lieutenant, I knew you were *capable* of passing; you knew your work better than some men whose political connections have made them captains. The question was whether you would try.

"It would have been easier had you failed. Whether the cause was deliberate choice or simple panic, I could have had you broken, and then you could have escaped with very little consequence. But you insisted on trying. Your brother was made midshipman, but *you* and no other made yourself a damned fine lieutenant." He sighed again, looking away from me. "Now it may have earned you a hanging."

His speech had produced such a muddle in me that I stood with my jaw loose. Granger had said to me at the time that I deserved the rank of lieutenant, but never had he spoken with such glowing praise. I had been prepared for his rage, even if he condemned me to execution. To receive an accolade instead left me staggering.

I could think of nothing to say. I expected hanging; I had no plans for avoiding it. Granger considered for several long minutes, then shook his head. "I don't see a solution, but that doesn't mean one can't be found. I received orders when we came into port: we leave again just as soon as we return to Plymouth. A short cruise only, perhaps two or three months. But to lose two of my three lieutenants now would be disastrous; it therefore follows that I must keep you both. By the time that is done, if no better answer has presented itself...." He sighed. "Then you will have to desert. And upon our return, I will make certain Byrom is condemned for what he has done."

From the standpoint of the greater good, it was success. Byrom would be kept away from any position that might allow him to lead others to their deaths, and I would escape with my life. But I would lose everything else I valued.

The service.

Harry.

Simon could hope to keep something of his friend, even after marriage. But with Simon gone, what could Victoria hope for? Charity might move Harry to correspond occasionally with his friend's invalid sister, but we could never meet. He would know me in an instant. And I could not bear to receive distant, cordial letters, when Harry had been closer to me than any save my own twin.

But my personal feelings did not signify. I had done what I must, and with that, I must be satisfied.

In the aftermath of my revelation to Granger, I wished at first that I might speak privately with Kate, without arousing her husband's suspicions. We had once been great friends, before her family shifted to Italy; together we had gotten ourselves into no end of trouble by dressing as boys—that being part of the reason it was thought better to school her in a foreign country—and surely, if I were to share my woes with anyone, it should be her. But Kate was out of my reach. And besides, it was not to her that I wished to unburden myself.

I found Harry avoiding the dancing—and, I rather suspected, his fiancée. What a fine pair we made: both of us miserable, for no cause we could publicly admit. He took gratefully to my suggestion that we walk outside. I could not tell him what troubled me, but at least I might take comfort in his company.

"I owe you an apology," I said as we left the lights and laughter of the house behind. "For what I said before, regarding Miss Fanning."

Harry shook his head, hands locked behind his back as if we paced the quarterdeck. "No, you were right to chide me. Such dishonesty was not fair to you, or to her."

"Dishonesty!" The word burst from me, carried on something that was almost a laugh. "You didn't lie, Harry. You simply… *postponed* a truth." The brief ripple of merriment faded quickly. "No, I can hardly condemn you for that. Not when I have done so much worse."

The admission was not one I had intended to make. Harry paused on the gravelled walk, turning curious surprise on me. "Whatever do you mean, Simon?"

I should never have begun on this topic; having started, I could not stop. No, it went back further than that. It became too late the moment I opened my mouth to Granger, and let the weight of Byrom's secret slip loose from where I had kept it stowed.

"I have lied to you, Harry. To everyone. I have no right lecture anyone on matters of honesty."

The startled silence that followed would not last, I knew. I had said too much. Harry could not possibly let the matter rest, not after that.

His reply, however, took my breath away. "I'm sure you had good reason."

Another impulse to laugh, though I was not amused in the slightest. "Oh, no. I wish I could say it was so. But my reason is nothing more than a despicable urge to preserve my own skin." Bitterness laced the admission, even more than I had shown in front of Granger.

We walked on another few steps. Then Harry's shoulders went back, and he raised his chin. "I know you, Simon, and I know you to be an honourable man. That is enough. You needn't say anything more. Whatever matter drove you to lie, you'll find no condemnation from me."

Warmth and pain alike burned me within. I had not looked for forgiveness, and did not deserve it in the slightest. Yet the fact that Harry gave it, unquestioning, made me feel—if only for the briefest of moments—that I had not, after all, lost everything I valued in the world.

If only he had not given that forgiveness to *Simon*. To an honourable *man*.

It should have been enough to shut my mouth. But my long stalemate with Byrom might as well have been a mist, that was at long last clearing from my vision, and with it gone I could see clearly once more. My own well-being did not matter in the slightest, when weighed against the damage that man could do, if given more authority and scope for his flaws. My impending desertion might discredit me, and therefore allow Byrom to escape censure for what happened to the *Persephone*, but sooner or later he would err again. And if others were on guard for it, he might yet be stopped.

Yes. I'd had enough of lying. Whatever the cost to me, the time had come to tell the truth.

"Harry, I'm a woman."

That…was not what I had intended to say.

I stopped, a pace after Harry did. How was it that my knees continued to hold me? The habits of battle, I supposed, that kept my body strong even when my mind was limp with fear. I could not bring myself to turn and see Harry's face. He said nothing, and the rest of the truth limped out of me, quieter and less passionate. "I'm not Simon. I'm Victoria."

A soft crunch of gravel from behind me, as if his weight had settled from the step he did not take. An exhalation of air, cut off, as if he began to say *How?* or something else to that effect, but could not finish the word.

I bowed my head. "Do you recall when you were all given leave, not long after Simon joined as a midshipman? He suffered a blow to his head when he fell while riding." My throat tightened, such that I had trouble going on. "The truth is that he died. The one who returned to the ship was not Simon, but me."

Six years. It would not take long for Harry to calculate the span for himself. He had known Simon, the *real* Simon, for a scant few months. The man he called friend was no man at all, but me.

Yet that friendship was real, and I owed it to him at least to meet his gaze. When I turned to face him, he shook his head, not blinking. "Why?"

"The inheritance," I said. Harry knew the situation well enough; he did not need it explained. Which was fortunate, as I could not have said more if I wanted to. Now, far too late, the enormity of what I had just done struck me. The captain had granted me one final cruise in which to plan my exit, but that was now impossible. I had managed, barely, to live with Byrom when he knew my secret; I could not do the same with Harry.

Which meant I would never return to the *Hesperides*.

Harry shook his head again. I'd seen men with similar expressions, after they suffered a blow to the head in battle. Dazed and uncomprehending. "Why tell me now?"

The unbinding of my true self let the anger loose, that I had tried to keep in check before Granger. With undisguised venom—both for Byrom and for myself—I related the truth of the *Persephone*'s demise, and the second lieutenant's subsequent blackmail. To this I added the admission that I had confessed to the captain, earlier that evening.

"And damn it all, it isn't *fair*," I burst out, when I thought I was finished. "I may hope to block his promotion at the very least, and surely his own flaws will damn him in time. With my word against his, though, I have little hope of his removal from the Navy. Not if I am revealed, or forced to flee. And why should *he* stay, when I must go? I am a hundred times the lieutenant he is!"

Harry's expression had closed down during my explanation, hiding his reactions behind an impassive wall. He looked up as I finished my tirade, though, and he nodded. "It's true. You have done very well. For a woman."

My heart twisted almost into a knot.

Then he added, very quietly, "Or even for a man."

His praise might be less fervent than Granger's, yet it meant so much more to me. Even that light, however, could barely touch the darkness that had settled over my spirit. "Much good may it do me," I said, as low as I had ever been. "If I don't wish to be court-martialled and hanged, I shall have to find some exit from the service, and likely it will be as a deserter. My only satisfaction will be that I have put a hole in Byrom's hull, to sink him in time."

"That, at least, I will be sure to see happen," Harry said, in a tone scarcely less intense than mine.

It strengthened me, to know I did not stand alone. "Thank you." I hesitated, wondering if Harry was now regretting the forgiveness he had offered, before I'd even told him the truth. I *had* to know. "I hope we may at least part as friends, on that count if no other."

Harry's reply was long enough in coming that I almost gave in to despair. But at last he nodded, not looking at me, and said, "Yes. S—Victoria—we are still friends."

It was not friendship I wanted from him. With the barrier of my deception stripped away, I could admit that to myself; I had loved him for years, as more than a mere companion. But I must release that now, as I had released all other hopes, and be grateful for what I might keep. His friendship, and the sound of his voice, addressing me at last by my true name.

I wished it felt less like a knife in my heart.

"What will you do?" he asked. "After you leave."

I aimed for an air of carelessness, and came at least within shot of it. "I will figure something out. My skills are many, if not those of a lady. Come, we should return to the party; your family and fiancée will be wondering where you have gone." I had not intended to mention Miss Fanning. Where had my restraint gone?

But Harry, it seemed, was as eager to escape this dreadful embarrassment as I was. Distracted, he said, "Yes. Let us go back. I have matters I must attend to."

The evening was nearly at an end, and I had drunk more than was wise. What else should I do, though? The waters in which I sailed had shallowed without warning; I was surrounded by shoals on every side. (And my imagination was determined to wallow in nautical metaphors, as if to rub salt in the wound of that loss.) Byrom and Granger and Mrs. Warrington and Kate and most of all....

Where had Harry gone?

I could not find him, nor Kate. In my search, however, I ran afoul of Byrom, who trapped me against one wall of the ballroom, malicious pleasure on his thin face. "You did well with those women, Ravenswood. Such a touching tale; I nearly wept to hear it. Perhaps I'll have you set it to music, next."

Staring into his calculating eyes, I found I could no longer recall why I was protecting his secret. What loss could I suffer, that I would not suffer regardless? My life? There seemed no reason why I should preserve it. The battle-madness that had made me speak the truth to Granger was back, but colder this time.

"I thought I might sell my story to a newspaper, instead," I told him, through a smile that could more rightly be called a baring of teeth. "Tales of blackmail always attract such prurient interest."

It took a moment for him to absorb my words. Then his own expression hardened into a snarl. "You know I can destroy you."

"And I, you," I answered. "A pretty impasse, is it not?"

Byrom scoffed. "No one will take your word for it. Not when

I expose you for what you are."

He did not know I had already told Granger and Harry. He did not know I had already embraced my fate, robbing his threat of its force. "Plenty of people will be willing to believe it when I expose you for what *you* are: a coward and an incompetent, unworthy of your rank, or even the name of gentleman."

His face purpled with rage. Through his teeth, he said, "If you weren't a worthless bitch, I'd call you out for that insult."

Now, far too late, Harry appeared. He had re-entered the ballroom with Kate, and was making his way past the dancers toward me. What had the two of *them* been doing together? It hardly mattered. "You don't dare face me, and you know it," I said.

Harry only heard my reply, but even a blind man could have seen the threat in the air. His hand closed around my arm. "Come with me, Simon. I need to speak with you, in private."

Was it habit that made him still call me Simon, or a friendly concern for my dying masquerade? It didn't matter. The name, I think, lit the final fuse, for Byrom knew it to be a lie. As Harry tried to drag my resisting body away, the second lieutenant laughed, making no attempt to quiet it. "Always together, Wycliffe, eh? Hoping to make him your catamite? You'll find a nasty surprise if you do."

All around us, conversation died.

Harry dropped my arm. Body taut as a line under tension, he turned to face Byrom fully. And I remembered, with fierce joy and sudden fear commingled, Harry's words on board the ship, before we came here. *I should like to see you call him out.*

I could not. But *Harry*....

His voice could carry over the roar of guns in battle; he only used a tenth of that volume now. It was enough. Everyone within a dozen paces heard him. "For that insult, *sir*, you will beg my pardon on your knees—or you will meet me on the field of honour."

Byrom licked his lips, a quick, nervous flick of the tongue. He had gone too far, and he knew it. He could provoke me all he liked, and I could not call him out for it; no man need accept a challenge from a woman. But he had always confined himself to that safe target, minding his tongue around those who might rightly demand satisfaction. My secret was no defence for him now: the public implication that Harry was a sodomite would stand regardless. And that challenge must be answered.

Lord Deverell had heard it. So had Kate. And Granger, too, who spoke into the silence. "Mr. Byrom. Your words are an insult no gentleman could accept. Will you apologise?"

The second lieutenant's gaze slid to me. I held my breath, wondering if he would do it regardless: expose me, simply for the vindictive pleasure of my destruction. But then his attention returned to Harry, and a thin smile spread across his lips. He had, I realised with leaden horror, found a better way to hurt me.

"I will not, sir."

The captain's tone was grim. "I dislike my officers to duel, but in this case, it seems unavoidable. Lord Deverell, I beg your pardon for this disruption. Although the law may often look the other way when gentlemen agree to settle their differences in combat, the practice *is* illegal. We will not trouble you—"

"Nonsense," our host boomed. Kate was by his side; had she whispered in his ear? I had not been watching her closely enough. "If the gentlemen are in accord—regarding the duel, that is; not in the matter of the insult—then I see no reason why they should not be allowed to resolve the matter as they see fit. And one really needs dry land for this sort of thing, not a ship's deck. I volunteer my terrace."

It was not the proper form; a duel should be delayed until the following day, to give heads time to cool. But with the *Hesperides* preparing to set sail again, there was justification for concluding the matter tonight, and Harry did not hesitate to take it up. "I thank you for your generosity, my lord. If Byrom concurs, I would be glad to face him now."

All eyes turned to the second lieutenant. The purple of anger had drained from his face, leaving him white, but he nodded stiffly. "I agree. Let it be done."

We swept toward the garden doors in a chattering crowd, Lord Deverell calling for a footman to bring his duelling pistols. Some of the ladies hung back, but others, Kate among them, came along. I could not spare any attention for her. To Harry I growled, "What are you *doing?* I did not ask you—"

"You didn't have to," Harry said, before I could finish. "I won't kill him—at least, I don't intend to. They'd put me on trial for that, and I'd be left ashore while I waited for the acquittal. But he deserves this, and we both know it."

Servants hung lamps to brighten the terrace, until it was as good as day out there. Fawcett, the Marine captain who had accompanied us to the party, stood as Byrom's second; he made no attempt to pretend he supported Byrom's cause, but honour demanded that *someone* observe the proper forms on his behalf. I, still reckless with my impending doom, declared myself Harry's second. Granger opened his mouth to object, then subsided, granting me this measure of vicarious satisfaction. Byrom's eyes promised murder for me, once he was done with Harry, but I no longer cared.

Fawcett and I agreed to the terms without difficulty. One pistol each, which we loaded under each other's supervision. The men would fire simultaneously at a distance of ten paces, and if one or both be disabled, the duel would end there.

I had seen Harry go into battle before, and feared for him, but never like this. However just his cause might be, this time, I could not fight at his side. If he should be wounded—God forbid, wounded badly....

I was not often given to praying, reasoning that God had little cause to favour a woman as impertinent as I. But I prayed now, that Harry be safe, and Byrom suffer the fate he deserved.

We gave the pistols to the duellists, and Lord Deverell himself counted off the paces. "You will turn on the count of three, and fire when I give the word, gentlemen."

Harry's eyes met mine, where I stood to one side. I should have spoken before this began—should have told him how I felt—we left too many things unsaid—

"One," Lord Deverell said. "Two."

As the word "three" left his mouth, Byrom spun and fired.

And something knocked me to the ground.

At first, my mind was an utter blank.

When at last I managed to form a thought, it was: *What a damnably stupid way out of my troubles.*

A babble of voices deafened me, words leaping clear in brief, half-comprehensible fragments. *Early—misfire—bad aim—cheating bastard—*And Byrom, claiming over and over again that it was an accident, that his gun had discharged as he turned, what shocking bad chance that I had been struck.

I pressed one hand to the spreading wetness on my coat. Lord Deverell was bellowing for Byrom to stand his ground and receive the return fire, and through a gap in the men now crowding around me, I saw Harry with his pistol outstretched.

"Harry," I said. It was soft, and could not possibly have carried over the noise of the crowd. But his head turned nonetheless. I met his gaze, and I shook my head. However much I despised Byrom—the murder I saw in his eyes before had been for me, not for his opponent; he had planned this from the start—I did not want Harry to kill him. He would be put on trial for murder, and even with an acquittal, the stain of that would follow him forever.

Harry's eyes returned to Byrom, and his lips peeled back in a snarl. Then he fired.

Byrom screamed. Through the legs around me, I saw him drop to the ground, clutching the shattered ruin of his knee. I had no doubt that Harry had struck what he aimed at.

Then I was being lifted and carried inside, while someone went for a doctor. It was all over, if not in the way I had expected; my secret would be lost entirely now. I rather wished Byrom had struck me somewhere more immediately lethal, so I would be spared the indignity that was about to come.

But no. I was laid on a sopha, and heard Kate's clear voice

giving orders. When the door shut, I was very nearly alone. The only ones who remained knew the truth, and were friends besides: Kate, and Granger, and Harry.

"My husband has a *lot* of money," Kate said, when I focussed my eyes on her. "Enough to buy one doctor's cooperation, certainly. And we three shall keep your secret."

Granger unbuttoned my coat with impersonal hands, then dragged up my shirt. The white corselet that flattened my meagre bosom showed clearly where Byrom's round had struck: my right side, just below my ribs. "I'm no doctor," he said, probing the wound, "but I think it missed your intestines. You have good odds of surviving this, Ravenswood."

"She had better," Kate said sharply. "I can't tell if you have spoiled our plan, Victoria, or played into it beautifully."

Plan? I remembered then what had preceded the insult and the duel: Kate and Harry, returning to the ballroom together. Like a pair of conspirators, ready to carry out their scheme.

Kate smiled at me. She could not entirely hide her worry, but it was mixed with a mad gleam I remembered from our childhood misadventures. "It goes like this. Miss Fanning has no more enthusiasm for her impending marriage than Lt. Wycliffe does. Familial pressure, however, prevents either one from admitting that openly. Now, the good lieutenant and I were not in agreement on the notion of faking your death, but as circumstances have presented us with this, ah, *opportunity*—"

She faltered, eyes going to my bloodstained body. Harry cleared his throat, and stepped into the breach. "If my good friend Simon were to beg me to look after his sister…I'm sure Miss Fanning would understand."

For one grinding, dreadful moment, I had a vision of myself as an invalid in truth, incapacitated by this wound, living as a spinster on the charity of Harry and his wife. But no, Kate had said something about lack of enthusiasm for the marriage. *Miss Fanning would understand….*

Oh.

The sudden acceleration of my heart could not be good for

my wound. Byrom disgraced, publicly, by his own hand, and now Harry was offering me—

No. It was *not* everything I had dreamed of. I closed my eyes, because I could not bear to let anyone see the shame there, the temptation to accept this crumb, because without it I had nothing. With so much else gone, I had only my dignity, and clung to it with all the strength I still retained. "I don't want your pity, Harry."

Above me, silence. And then he spoke. "It isn't pity. It's...." A pause, in which I thought my heart had stopped beating entirely. "It's affection."

I opened my eyes then, and met his, and saw in them what he had concealed under the shock of our earlier conversation: a mirror to my own feelings.

Feelings he could not admit then; it would not have been right, with him sworn to wed another. He should not admit them now. But that single word was more than enough. We were not simply friends, as he had said in the garden; we had not been *simply* friends for years, even if my masculine facade had forced us to call our bond by that name, or to divert it sideways into brotherhood. I knew, suddenly, that he remembered the near-kiss the night I was made lieutenant.

Harry blinked, and I realised from the burning in my own eyes that I had been staring into his for some untold moment. My tongue, working once more, gave voice to a laugh. "It's fitting, I suppose, given my strange life, that I should be proposed to while bleeding on Kate's sopha."

"It is not *quite* a proposal," Kate corrected me, after Harry and I had gazed at each other for another eternity. "We must put it about first that you have died, or rather that Simon has, and then Miss Fanning can release Lt. Wycliffe. But there must be no *actual* dying on your part, do you understand?"

"Yes," I agreed, not looking away from Harry. It was hard to speak; my lips wanted to stay stretched in a smile forever. "No dying."

How could I die? I suddenly had all the reason in the world to live.

✳

I played the part of the invalid passably well, I think, courtesy of Byrom's cowardly shot, and my subsequent long recovery. The wedding was small, out of consideration for my supposed weakness—much greater in story than in truth. It was just as well: fewer guests meant fewer people to wonder at the bride's oddly weathered face, or less-than-graceful bearing in her gown.

Afterward, Harry and I walked in the garden of his family's house. A breeze was blowing, and out of habit I raised my head and inhaled deeply. But the air carried no hint of salt.

Harry did not miss the sudden melancholy in my expression. "You miss it, don't you."

I sighed. "I miss a great many things. For all its bad parts— the danger, and the brutality, and the restrictions of shipboard life—I felt honoured to be in the service. More than anything, though, I miss the sea."

My new husband took my hand in his own. "There are benefits to this peace with France, you know. Unlike a great many lieutenants, I face no hardship in being put off and placed on half pay. And there are a great many opportunities for a trained officer, outside the service." He looked to the south, toward the distant sea. "Some of those opportunities are much more... *flexible*."

As with his proposal—as with so many of the things he said—Harry left his precise meaning unspoken. I heard it well enough. My breath drew in, calling only the faintest of twinges from my side. "You mean—"

He nodded. My hand tightened on his: still a strong grip, despite my convalescence, and the callouses remained, under my glove. Would the crew of a merchant vessel put up with their captain's wife interfering in shipboard affairs? Surely we could assemble one that would.

I had not lost the sea.

Smiling fit to crack my face in half, I walked on with my husband through the garden, the wind gusting in my ears with a sound like waves.

DYING OLD

STRYCHNINE IS BITTER, but the most pleasant to work with. Small enough doses show no effect; indeed, your physician agrees your digestion is better after you begin your work with the poison. Only once do you miscalculate, and the tremors that shake your body leave your heart racing long after the strychnine's effects have faded. It reminds you how easy it would be for this to go wrong—for you to cut your own life short, rather than armouring it against those who would do so themselves.

Arsenic is mild, leaving only an aftertaste of sweetness, and sometimes a metallic sensation as well. But it yellows your skin and makes your hair fall out, gives you burning pains in your hands and your feet. The man advising you swears this is expected, and will not kill you. You almost have him executed anyway. How simple would it be for your enemies to buy this man's loyalty? Then all the world would laugh at Mithridates, who took his own life through foolishness and hubris. But the man knows what will happen to him if you perish; therefore you trust him, and continue on, until arsenic no longer troubles you.

Cyanide makes you gasp as if the gods had taken the air away. If you did not doubt the man before, you do so now, when the world spins and your heart pounds and your stomach twists as if it would tear itself apart. But you made up your mind to trust him, and if you were wrong, it is too late now to undo your error. Your breath returns; the world becomes stable once more; afterward you smile when you catch the scent of almonds.

Nightshade dries your mouth and blurs your vision, showing you things that are not there. Hemlock weakens your muscles, until you feel helpless as a babe. Oleander you vomit up, again and again, but each time the dose you expel is larger; it is progress, even if your body never becomes indifferent to it.

And over time, you begin to laugh. All the toxins of the world, and none of them can kill you. This work becomes rumour, gossip, challenge; of course men decide to test it. You recognize the strange odour of mandrake, the burning touch of daphne, the pleasant taste of death cap mushrooms—but none of them trouble you. Indeed, you have achieved your aim: you cannot die by poison.

In exchange, you have spent your years in misery. Trembling, aching, spewing your guts out more times than you can count. Your hair is thin and brittle, your skin mottled with discolourations and rash. Your joints ache as you move, though you have not yet reached your dotage. Nightmares plague you when you sleep and visions haunt you by day, ghosts of horrors and things too strange for words. You laugh, but you cannot remember a time when you faced a meal with joy.

Well done, O king. You have made yourself a legend and a twisted thing. Many will die, thinking to follow your example; those who do not may regret it.

And when you die—not of poison, not directly, but perhaps of their effects over the long and wretched years—you will welcome it with relief.

AFTERWORD

Before May of 2006, I had never attempted to write historical fiction. But it would not quite be true to say I had never attempted to tell a story set in history: in January of that year I began running a tabletop role-playing game, using the *Changeling: The Dreaming* system and setting, which took the characters backward through six hundred and fifty years of London's past. And in the course of running that game, I discovered something:

Historical fiction is *really fun.*

Writing it is kind of a game in its own right. They say constraint feeds creativity; history provides both constraint and fuel. If you're trying to tell a story that fits seamlessly into the frame of the past, either because it's non-speculative or because the fantasy elements are slipped in as secret elements, then you can't just change things willy-nilly. I've lost count of the times when I gnashed my teeth over real-world events refusing to line up with my plots. On the other hand, I've also lost count of the times when history handed me the perfect little detail on a silver platter. To pick but one example out of the stories in this collection, the entire concept of "The Damnation of St. Teresa of Ávila" grew out of a coincidence of timing, her passing coinciding with the switch to the Gregorian calendar, when the calendar jumped forward ten days. I would never think that up for a tale set in a secondary world: it's too random. I needed history to make that story happen.

Writing historical fiction or historical fantasy is also, of course, a lot of work. When I was working on the Onyx Court series of novels, I referred to them—tongue only slightly in cheek—as my home Ph.D. in English history. I had a small bookcase where I kept my research materials; the reference works for the fourth novel, *With Fate Conspire*, filled all three shelves. For a short story, one generally does not go so far…but I read an entire academic book on the Gunpowder Plot for "And Blow Them at the Moon," and the only reason I didn't have to read more was that I already knew the period pretty well from having written *Midnight Never Come* (set a couple of decades prior) and *In Ashes Lie* (set a couple of decades later). The research-to-finished-work ratio is often appalling enough that it's safer not to think about it.

The end result, though, can feel like gears clicking smoothly together, the factual and the fanciful interlocking until it's hard to believe they weren't meant to mesh like that. I titled this collection *Ars Historica*, which is Latin for "the historical art," because writing this type of story does really feel like a specialized art form. Its challenges and rewards bring me back, time and again.

And that concludes my general remarks. For commentary on the individual stories, read on.

STORY NOTES

Notes on "And Blow Them at the Moon"

If I class novellas as something other than short fiction, this is the first piece of Onyx Court short fiction I ever wrote. If you choose to read the currently extant stories from that series in chronological order (which you can do in the omnibus *In London's Shadow*), it takes place after *Midnight Never Come*, and before the novella *Deeds of Men* (which was the first piece I wrote between the novels).

Most of my ideas for Onyx Court side stories come from specific individuals or events in history. If my faeries are meddling in mortal affairs, then it's only natural to ask: what did they do when *this* was going on? But that poses an immediate challenge, because I don't want to take agency away from the people who made those things happen in reality. Sometimes it's easy to slip my faeries into the gaps; the Spanish Armada, for example, was defeated by a number of human-driven factors, but also by some really unfortunate weather. I have no compunctions about giving my faeries credit for the storms.

But it gets more difficult when you're dealing with something like the Gunpowder Plot, which was human action from one end to the other. According to my self-imposed rules, a faerie character could not be the real instigator of the plot. Nor could they stop it in a way that negated the efforts of real people. How could I fit them in?

The answer to that question took a premise that could have

been simple action and intrigue, and made it much more tragic than I anticipated. In doing my research, I was deeply moved by the ethical and spiritual conundrum Father Garnet faced. It's easy for me to say he should have warned people; I'm a modern American, raised Methodist but in practice an agnostic, and the seal of the confessional gets filed under "a nice idea" in my brain. *Okay, sure, you shouldn't go sharing people's secrets—but when we're talking about an actual criminal conspiracy...*In order to write this story, I had to put myself in Father Garnet's shoes, had to understand why that sacred obligation meant so much to him that he risked not only his own life, but those of other people, in order to uphold it.

And then—because writers are sadists—I had to put Magrat in the desperate and doomed position of trying to save him.

In the end, her connection to the Gunpowder Plot is more personal than political. The one point of direct intervention I gave her is the so-called Monteagle Letter. We don't actually know who wrote it, though Tresham, Salisbury, and Lord Monteagle himself have all been tagged as suspects; that made it a prime opening for faerie interference. (Honesty compels me to note that the implied criticism of Magrat's ability to write is a cover for the fact that I decided not to modernize the spelling or punctuation of the original text. To a reader in the early seventeenth century, that would have looked perfectly normal.) The rest is about her own internal conflict and the choices *she* makes, in a period where a lot of other people were making extremely bad—or at least tragic—choices of their own.

Sometimes there are no happy endings.

"And Blow Them at the Moon" was originally published in issue #50 of *Beneath Ceaseless Skies*, in August 2010.

NOTES ON "THE DEATHS OF CHRISTOPHER MARLOWE"

I said in my Afterword that I first attempted to write historical fiction in May of 2006. This is the story I wrote.

It came about because I found a website that proposed a fascinating theory. Nearly a decade later, I can't remember the specifics very well, but the writer used a couple of historical documents to suggest a possible connection between a foreigner named Le Doux and Christopher Marlowe, who had died—or at least been declared dead—two years earlier. It was a lovely theory...until I hit the postscript added by the writer, wherein he shamefacedly admitted that it didn't hold up, that he'd misinterpreted something and, in light of the correct interpretation, his nice little web of evidence fell apart.

That was my introduction to the micro-genre of Marlovian murder conspiracies. There are a surprising number of them, for a guy who died (or didn't die?) more than four hundred years ago. And the thing about conspiracy theories is, they're *fun*. They're little intellectual puzzles, challenging you to create a framework in which all the disparate facts form a cool picture. You don't have to believe in them as literal truth to find beauty in the process— though I have to admit that the more you look at them, the more they start to *make sense*....

In the end, none of them were wholly persuasive to me. (And I do mean none: the official story of his death has enough oddities and coincidences in it to make me raise an eyebrow.) Which is why, when I set out to write a Marlowe story, I ended up exploring several possible iterations, and not handing down a ruling on any of them. Wrong theory or no, I am indebted to that unknown online writer: his website gave me the material I needed for this tale, from an outline of various competing theories to the original documents I have quoted throughout.

"The Deaths of Christopher Marlowe" was originally published in issue #12 of *Paradox*, in April of 2008.

✳

NOTES ON "TWO PRETENDERS"

This story was written in 2010, and it has an odd connection to the earthquake in Haiti that year: fans on LiveJournal organized a community auction, and one of the items I offered was an Onyx Court story, involving the historical personage or event of the winner's choice.

The recipient requested the Princes in the Tower, which put me in an odd position. You see, there *was* no Onyx Court at that point in time. The disappearance (and probable murder) of King Edward V and his younger brother Richard, Duke of York took place before the Onyx Hall and its associated court were created. But I could still write a story about faeries and the Princes, and with the permission of my recipient, that is what I did. (As for whether it's an Onyx Court story anyway: I consider it to be in the same continuity as those works, although there is no direct connection between them.)

Lambert Simnel and Perkin Warbeck were, of course, real people. They weren't the only pretenders to the throne in the wake of the Wars of the Roses, but they were two of the more memorable and successful ones—which made them prime candidates for inclusion in the story. All it took was a jaunt through Faerie, and lo, the pretenders became real.

"Two Pretenders" was originally published (with permission of the auction winner) in issue #60 of *Beneath Ceaseless Skies*, in January of 2011.

✳

NOTES ON "THE DAMNATION OF ST. TERESA OF ÁVILA"

I owe my husband credit for the existence of this story—or perhaps "blame" would be a more appropriate word. After all, it's his fault I wound up reading three-quarters of the saint's autobiography, and some of her other mystical writings as well.

He's the one who told me about the coincidence of timing, the saint passing away on the night when the calendar made its shift from Julian to Gregorian. I don't think he suggested what the significance of that should be—only that it ought to mean *something*. I filed the notion away in the back of my brain, and never expected anything to come of it.

That changed when Steven Diamond asked me for a story to put in his anthology *Shared Nightmares*. The idea I originally came up with wasn't working; I couldn't make it fit the anthology's horror tone without treating non-binary gender as a disturbing and wrong thing, which I did *not* want to do. (That idea eventually became "The Mirror-City," which you can find in my collection *Maps to Nowhere*. I therefore opened up my list of unused story concepts to look for an alternative. And lo, St. Teresa was waiting, years after I first thought of writing about her.

Let me be clear: I think she was a remarkable woman, and her achievements are worthy of tremendous respect. But when I started reading up on her theology, the "horror" angle pretty much wrote itself: she flat-out makes statements to the effect of "God only hurts me to show the depth of his love for me," which is more or less indistinguishable from the rhetoric of an abuse victim. There's plenty of excellent academic work that puts her ideas in context—everything from the Catholic valorization of suffering to the strategies by which a sixteenth-century woman navigated the control of her male superiors—but for this story, I chose to take an angle that says her agonizing experiences were *not* God's will, but her own.

I wish I could go back in time and make her life less painful—and I know she would probably refuse my aid if I tried.

"The Damnation of St. Teresa of Ávila" was published in *Shared Nightmares*, edited by Steven Diamond and Nathan Shumate, in November 2014.

✳

NOTES ON "TO RISE NO MORE"

Ada Lovelace is one of those awesome historical figures who deserves to have more stories written about her. She was the daughter of Lord Byron, the famously passionate poet, and Annabella Milbanke, a female mathematician; she was friends with Charles Babbage, inventor of the Difference Engine and the Analytical Engine; owing her work on the latter, she is often called the world's first computer programmer.

When I wrote *With Fate Conspire*, the fourth book of the Onyx Court series, I wanted to include Ada in it somehow. After all, there's a device in the novel that is directly inspired by the Analytical Engine. But that story takes place in 1884, and Ada died (sadly quite young) in 1852. Fortunately for me, all of the Onyx Court books have a scattering of flashback scenes, so all I needed to do was read up on her and see whether her life offered any hooks upon which I might hang a connection to the faeries.

Oh my *god* did it ever.

Ada referred to herself as Babbage's "fairy helper." She talked about how she could draw on resources others didn't know about. And yes: as a young girl, she tried to build a pair of wings to fly with. I made up Alarch, but every other detail of Ada's obsession with flight is absolutely real. Because history is cooler than you could hope for, and sometimes hands you the perfect details on a plate.

Having put her into that flashback, of course I wanted to write a story that focused on her directly, and how she came to be connected with the Onyx Court. The whole "wings" thing seemed the perfect direction to go in…but she never succeeded in that quest. (What she wanted to do is physically impossible anyway, without either magic or much more advanced engineering than she had available to her.) So I had to extend my tale further down her timeline, past the illness that left her bedridden for years, to the moment when she re-entered the world of impossible dreamers—which is to say, the day she met Charles Babbage.

It's a tradition with Onyx Court stories to draw both the title and any epigraphs from literature of the period. Naturally I had to use a piece of Lord Byron's; he was kind enough to oblige me with something quite topical.

"To Rise No More" was published in issue #207 of *Beneath Ceaseless Skies*, in September of 2016.

NOTES ON "FALSE COLOURS"

It's no secret that the Onyx Court series of novels are based (to varying degrees, depending on which part of the series you look at) on the *Changeling: The Dreaming* game I mentioned in my Afterword. But those aren't the only game experiences I've turned into fiction; this story is another one.

The tale of "Simon" Ravenswood is one of my favorite examples of how games can, when you least expect it, produce a moment of serendipitous beauty. The game in question was a one-shot LARP (short for "live action role-playing"—think of it as improv theatre), set in the Regency era, and based around a house party to which the characters had all been invited. The game was full of intrigue and magic…but as it happened, one of the players fell sick and didn't show up. And his character was the one who was tied in with the disappearance of Victoria's brother, which had to do with various magical conspiracies involving other groups in the game.

Because that player wasn't there, I had *no bloody clue* there were magical conspiracies running around. My experiences were wholly mundane: I was worried about my nemesis, a fellow lieutenant who knew my true identity; my love interest, a fellow lieutenant who did not; and my childhood best friend, the hostess of the party, who recognized me and immediately started meddling. I suffered melodramatic agonies over telling lies to the family of a dead midshipman, confessed the truth of that wreck to my captain, and wound up blurting out my real identity to my love interest when I just couldn't take it anymore. And there I expected matters to rest, because the game was going to end soon, and my love interest was, after all, pledged elsewhere.

While I was busy enjoying my personal drama, the conspiracies were going haywire. I wound up trying to block the doors when most of the characters in the game began stampeding around, chasing an invisible doctor-turned-spy who had stolen some magical macguffin-or-other—seriously, to this day I can't tell you what was going on there. I only know that my captain, who could see the invisible guy, tried to shoot him and missed. And then he tried again, and missed again…and this time, when the player mimed his action, his arm was pointed directly at me.

So of course I asked the woman in charge of the game whether that meant *I* got shot instead.

We played rock-paper-scissors to see if I did (this being a common resolution mechanic in live-action games), me wondering all the while if I should just relent. We tied, and then I *did* relent: friends later said that any female character cross-dressing as a man ought to lose on ties to avoid getting wounded, just because that's such a time-honored trope for this kind of tale. And so I was shot by my own captain…mere seconds after my love interest and my best friend came into the room, fresh from plotting how they were going to fake my death to solve all my problems.

Nobody scripted this. It just happened. I didn't know they were plotting to fake my death; I didn't know I was going to get shot; it was all a series of beautiful coincidences.

Which is why I asked their permission to turn those events into a story someday. It took me years to do so, and when I did, a lot of details changed; while it may be hilarious to have no clue there's a giant plot going on elsewhere during a game, it makes for some weird and probably unsuccessful fiction. I had to restructure things to make the various conflicts line up—in the game, Byrom slunk off to be ignominiously cashiered after the finale, which wouldn't have been very satisfying here—and weave in various loose ends. But the inspiration is still very much there, and I am indebted to those friends for both a splendid game, and the story that resulted.

"False Colours" was originally published in *Wilful Impropriety: 13 Tales of Society and Scandal*, edited by Ekaterina Sedia, in April 2012.

NOTES ON "DYING OLD"

Like "Two Pretenders," this story began life as a gift. But in this case, the context was entirely different: the 2012 Yuletide fanfiction exchange.

Yuletide has a *very* broad definition of fanfiction, you see, and it includes what in a professional context would simply be called historical fiction. One of the requests that year was for a story about Mithridates VI of Pontus, the king immortalized in A.E. Houseman's *A Shopshire Lad*:

> There was a king reigned in the East:
> There, when kings will sit to feast,
> They get their fill before they think
> With poisoned meat and poisoned drink.
> He gathered all that springs to birth
> From the many-venomed earth;
> First a little, thence to more,
> He sampled all her killing store;
> And easy, smiling, seasoned sound,
> Sate the king when healths went round.
> They put arsenic in his meat
> And stared aghast to watch him eat;
> They poured strychnine in his cup
> And shook to see him drink it up:

They shook, they stared as white's their shirt:
Them it was their poison hurt.
—I tell the tale that I heard told.
Mithridates, he died old.

I set out to write a story about his efforts to inoculate himself against poison…but when I began researching the kinds of things he might have consumed, I hit a litany of the unfortunate physical effects produced by sub-lethal doses. By the time I was done describing them, the end of the story was inevitable, as was the title.

"Dying Old" was originally posted on An Archive of Our Own, in December 2012.

ABOUT THE AUTHOR

MARIE BRENNAN is a former anthropologist and folklorist who shamelessly pillages her academic fields for inspiration. She most recently misapplied her professors' hard work to *The Night Parade of 100 Demons*, a *Legend of the Five Rings* novel, and *The Mask of Mirrors*, the first book of the Rook and Rose trilogy (jointly written with Alyc Helms as M.A. Carrick). Her Victorian adventure series The Memoirs of Lady Trent was a finalist for the Hugo Award; the first book of that series, *A Natural History of Dragons*, was a finalist for the World Fantasy Award. Her other works include the Doppelganger duology, the urban fantasy Wilders series, the Onyx Court historical fantasies, the Varekai novellas, and nearly sixty short stories, as well as the *New Worlds* series of worldbuilding guides. For more information, visit swantower.com, her Twitter @swan_tower, or her Patreon at www.patreon.com/swan_tower.

ABOUT BOOK VIEW CAFÉ

Book View Café Publishing Cooperative (BVC) is an author-owned cooperative of professional writers, publishing in a variety of genres such as fantasy, romance, mystery, and science fiction.

BVC authors include New York Times and USA Today best-sellers; Nebula, Hugo, and Philip K. Dick Award winners; World Fantasy Award and Campbell Award nominees; and winners and nominees of many other publishing awards.

Since its debut in 2008, BVC has gained a reputation for producing high-quality e-books, and is now bringing that same quality to its print editions.